THE HOUSE AT

Belle Fontaine

STORIES

THE HOUSE AT

Belle Fontaine

STORIES

LILY TUCK

Atlantic Monthly Press
New York

These stories originally appeared in the following publications:

"The House at Belle Fontaine" in *The American Scholar*; "Lucky" in *The Kenyon Review*; "St. Guilhem-le-Désert" in a different form in *Ploughshares*; "My Flame" in *The Yale Review*; "Bloomsday in Bangkok" in a different form in *Fiction*; "My Music" in *Alaska Quarterly Review*; "Ice" in *The American Scholar* and in *The PEN/O. Henry Prize Stories 2011*; "The Riding Teacher" in *Epoch*; "Pérou" in *Epoch* and in the *PEN/O. Henry Prize Stories 2013*; and "Sure and Gentle Words" in *The Yale Review*

Published simultaneously in Canada
Printed in the United States of America

FIRST EDITION

ISBN-13: 978-0-8021-2016-8

Atlantic Monthly Press
an imprint of Grove/Atlantic, Inc.
841 Broadway
New York, NY 10003

Distributed by Publishers Group West

www.groveatlantic.com

13 14 15 16 17   10 9 8 7 6 5 4 3 2 1

To Frances Kiernan

Contents

THE HOUSE AT

Belle Fontaine

STORIES

The House at Belle Fontaine

Monsieur Rossier has asked Ella to dinner at a quarter past seven on a Saturday night in late February. Monsieur Rossier, her landlord, is very old and very rich—one of the richest men in France, she has heard people say. He is also alone. He lives in a large château, which he built in the Norman style, with broad, dark, exterior beams that are ugly and out of place in that part of the country, while the stucco house that Ella rents from him is old; a portion of it dates back to the eighteenth century, with ivy growing up its lopsided but graceful yellow walls. Ella's house is set in a garden with a pretty fountain—*belle fontaine*—and there are tall chestnut trees that form an allée and bloom white in the spring. Her house is lovelier than Monsieur Rossier's château but, like him, she feels lonely in it, particularly that winter in the north of France, when it rains a lot and is cold.

During the time that Ella and her children live in the house called Belle Fontaine—a time when little occurs and her life seems at a standstill—Ella is a bit frightened of Monsieur Rossier, even though he is old and frail, and she is always afraid that he will find fault with her as a tenant. She wants him to approve of her, to like her even, although it is quite clear to Ella that they can never be friends. The age and, more important, the social barrier is too large. Still, Ella admires what she calls Monsieur Rossier's old-world standards and his outmoded courtliness and she also worries about him—for instance, when, for several weeks, he does not come out to his château and, instead, stays in Paris on account of the weather or, worse, his health. And each time this happens and she asks after him, the men who work for him—the maître d'hôtel, the gardener, the gatekeeper—shake their heads and tell Ella that it is a miracle he is alive at all.

On the first Friday of each month, his health and the weather permitting, Monsieur Rossier pays Ella a call. He comes to collect the rent and read the electric meter—or, rather, she reads it for him because he cannot see the little numbers jumping in the box. And, since he arrives in the late afternoon, Ella builds a fire in the living room and makes tea and they sit together while he figures out in his shaky, spidery handwriting how much Ella owes him and then she, in turn, writes him out a check, careful not to make a mistake or to misspell the numbers in French, for she does not want him to think her careless or irresponsible. Once Ella gives him the check, Monsieur Rossier relaxes visibly and settles himself more comfortably in his chair. He drinks the weak, sweetened tea Ella gives him and talks to her in his correct but accented English about the bad weather, the difficulty of finding good men to work on his property now that times have changed so, and, invariably, he talks about the past. And Ella sits and listens and tries to show genuine interest in his problems and in his memories. She nods and shakes her head and says yes and no at the appropriate moments, although she knows it really does not matter what she says, because Monsieur Rossier is not listening or paying attention to her.

One event only stands out during the first months she lived at Belle Fontaine—although it had nothing to do with Ella personally and it happened when she and the children had just arrived and were barely settled in the house—and it is terrible. On a clear Sunday morning in September, several minutes after take-off, a DC-10 carrying 315 passengers crashed a few kilometers south of the château into the forest of Ermenonville, killing everyone on board. According to reports, one of the cargo doors had not shut properly, and this led to a sudden loss of cabin pressure, which also caused part of the flooring to collapse, and this in turn damaged the controls of the plane. All day, from her house, Ella heard the wail of sirens. The roads were closed to traffic and in the village the pretty thirteenth-century Romanesque church was turned into a makeshift morgue. For days, the people in the village talked of nothing else; Ella's children, too, spoke of it nonstop, the youngest child swearing tearfully that he would never fly again. Morbid stories circulated. The plane had burned a mile-long trail through the forest, leaving blackened tree stumps. Monsieur Rossier's maître d'hôtel claimed he had seen the smoke from the wrecked plane on his way back from Mass, and he told Ella that people found limbs stuck in trees, a child's tiny foot inside a milk pail.

Then, since many passengers on that flight had been Japanese, the village was suddenly filled with Asian mourners. They arrived the following day in a caravan of minibuses, holding bouquets of flowers and looking vacant-eyed as they stumbled on the cobblestone streets on their way to the church. Ella noticed a young woman holding a child by the hand, who, despite yet another clear, sunny day, was wearing a yellow slicker similar to the ones her own children wore in the rain. The wife and child of a passenger, Ella guessed. At the sight of them, her eyes had filled with sudden hot tears and for a moment, standing there watching them, Ella imagined that she, too, had lost a loved one.

Twice, Monsieur Rossier has called to say he is expecting her at a quarter past seven and Ella is determined to arrive for dinner exactly on time. She will be punctual no matter what, she has told herself sternly and tonight she has no excuse—the children are away for the weekend, visiting their father, and the babysitter is off as well. Also, to avoid last-minute indecisions, she has already chosen what she will wear: a pleated skirt and silk blouse with her good pearl necklace, so that if Monsieur Rossier notices he will approve, for Ella will look like countless French ladies he has met, talked to and perhaps flirted with. The thought of Monsieur Rossier flirting makes Ella smile. Only he would never have flirted with her—of that Ella is quite sure—for she is an American, a foreigner and, worse, she is divorced. But now, of course, it no longer matters. And, also, Ella is so shy and constrained with him, she never makes a demand or complains about the house she rents, its inefficient single toilet, the leaky faucets, the lack of heat and the impractical, old-fashioned kitchen where, for instance, the sink is so low, she gets a backache from doing the dishes.

At seven o'clock sharp, dressed in the skirt and silk blouse and wearing her pearls and her city coat, Ella goes out the back door and opens the heavy iron gate, which is usually kept shut, as it separates Ella's garden from Monsieur Rossier's château and land. Outside, it is dark and cold; a ground fog has set in so that, after only a few steps, Ella can no longer see her house or the drawing room light she has deliberately left on, regardless of the electric bill. The château is not far—less than half a mile along a track that skirts a field—yet suddenly she is afraid and she is tempted to turn back to Belle Fontaine. She can go by car down the allée bordered by chestnut trees, then out to the main road and back around through Monsieur Rossier's gates and driveway. But she had thought it more sporty and neighborly to walk. Now, only her fear of being late makes her continue quickly in the dark until, at last, she can see the château silhouetted in front of her. The fog has blurred the outlines and the château looks like a part of the night sky, suspended on a bank of clouds, and almost beautiful.

As Ella's heels crunch in the driveway, a dog comes rushing out at her and starts to bark. She knows the dog—he belongs to the gatekeeper—and she speaks

sternly to him in French to show that she is not frightened, but the dog continues to run around her and bark.
When Ella reaches the château, she runs up the steps
while the dog remains below in the driveway, barking.
In the dark, Ella feels the wall with her hand for the
doorbell, and it occurs to her that maybe she has made
a mistake and the dinner is the following week. When
no one comes to the door, she starts to panic and wants
to go back, but she knows that the dog will not let her.
She is about to shout when, miraculously, the door opens
and she sees light and Monsieur Rossier.

"Good evening," he says. "I thought I heard someone coming up the steps but it's only ten past seven."

Is he reproaching her? "Good evening, monsieur,"
she says meekly as she slips off her coat. The maître
d'hôtel takes the coat from her. Seeing him in his white
serving jacket and white gloves, she does not recognize
him right away; he is more familiar to her in his blue
apron washing Monsieur Rossier's car and exchanging
gossip over the gate that divides their property. Tonight,
when she says, "*Bonsoir,*" he merely nods.

Ella follows Monsieur Rossier as he opens the door
into a room that is brightly lit and where a fire is blaz-
ing. Except for the dark television cabinet standing in a
corner, the room is mainly red, not just on account of the
fire but on account of the furniture, which is upholstered

in red leather. The curtains, too, are a red print fabric and, altogether, Ella likes the effect.

"Sit down, sit down, make yourself comfortable," Monsieur Rossier says.

Ella sits in a red leather armchair to one side of the fireplace. She wants the evening to be a success, and she will make an effort to be good company for the old man.

Monsieur Rossier offers Ella an aperitif. "A whiskey?" he asks.

"Unlike most Americans, I don't drink whiskey," Ella says, trying to make a joke.

"A glass of sherry then?" Frowning, Monsieur Rossier goes to a tray that has been set up with bottles, glasses and a bowl of ice and pours her the sherry.

Ella thanks him and half-raises her glass. "To your health," she says, but since Monsieur Rossier does not acknowledge her gesture, she lowers her glass.

Slowly, Monsieur Rossier settles himself into the red leather armchair facing hers by the fire and says, "This is my favorite room, especially on long, cold winter nights when I tend to feel a bit lonely."

Ella nods.

"But I really cannot complain," Monsieur Rossier continues, "my son who lives in London is very attentive."

"Your son lives in London?" Ella says. She has already been told that Monsieur Rossier's son lives in

London, but she is determined to keep the conversation going.

"Yes, my only son. He married an Englishwoman, and they have four boys. They come and spend Christmas here, it's a tradition, but otherwise they have their own lives. Their own friends. And they are too busy to visit an old man." Monsieur Rossier shrugs and smiles and Ella smiles back. "Here, let me show you their picture." With an effort, Monsieur Rossier gets up from his chair and goes to a table where he takes a silver-framed photograph of four young men—who look to be in their twenties, not much younger than she is—and he hands the photograph to Ella.

"They are very handsome," Ella says. She says it in such a way that it sounds as if she does not think so, but in fact she does. Embarrassed, she asks, "What are their names?"

"Yves, Didier, James and William," Monsieur Rossier recites, taking the photograph back from her. "You see, the parents compromised—half French, half English."

Ella says, "My children too—" but Monsieur Rossier interrupts her. "My son is really very good to me. He telephones every Sunday from London and he comes to Paris quite frequently on business and then we have lunch together."

Ella is about to say something when the maître d'hôtel opens the door, another door, leading directly into the dining room, and announces that dinner is served. Instead, she puts her half-empty glass of sherry on the table and takes another quick look at Monsieur Rossier's grandsons in the photograph.

Many years ago, Monsieur Rossier must have been tall and good-looking; now he is so shrunken and bent, he is not much taller than Ella; his hand shakes as he guides her into the next room where the maître d'hôtel stands, impassive, holding the door open for them. The dining room is vast and empty. The long table is covered with a blue linen cloth and has too many chairs around it. A bright overhead electric candelabra illuminates the bareness, and it makes Ella sad to think of Monsieur Rossier sitting here alone three times a day. How much nicer, if he were served on a tray in the sitting room in front of the fire, but that would no doubt be going against tradition or his principles. Monsieur Rossier motions Ella to the head of the table and she starts to sit down as, behind her, the maître d'hôtel holds out her chair. The thought crosses Ella's mind that he might pull the chair out from under her—a practical joke—and she has a hard time suppressing a giggle that unexpectedly wells up in her throat.

Monsieur Rossier hands her a printed menu. "Our dinner," he says.

Ella takes the menu: *paupiettes de veau* and *soufflé à la vanille*. Without comment, she hands the menu back to Monsieur Rossier—at least, she tells herself, she can look forward to the dessert.

The maître d'hôtel is at her side with a platter filled with white mounds—rice with a tomato sauce on the side. Carefully, Ella serves herself a mound. "*Merci,*" she tells the maître d'hôtel—she does not want him to think that she has no table manners—but he does not respond. He goes over to Monsieur Rossier with the platter of rice.

"Normally," Monsieur Rossier says, "I eat a light supper in the evening—a bowl of soup, cheese and a bit of fruit. It is not good for my digestion to eat a great deal in the evening. I am making an exception tonight."

No wonder the maître d'hôtel ignores her. He has to cook and serve a big meal instead of the usual soup and cheese and he will be in the kitchen much later than usual washing up and he will no doubt complain.

Ella eats the rice without tasting it. "Last week, when I was in Paris, I went to the theater," she says, determined to show Monsieur Rossier that she is capable of proper conversation, and, also, that she does not just sit around the house all day but has an active social and cultural life of her own. "I saw a play by Chekhov. It was set in modern times," she continues even after she sees that Monsieur Rossier, absorbed with his rice and eating it greedily, is not listening to her. A few grains of rice are stuck to the side of his mouth.

The maître d'hôtel pours water into her glass and then wine into her second glass. Ella takes a sip of her wine, which is very good. Monsieur Rossier, she notices, does not take any wine, only water.

When the old man raises his head and looks over at her, Ella can see that he is somewhere else far away. "I am so pleased you like Belle Fontaine," he says. Her mouth full of rice, Ella nods. She is not sure what he means. The way Monsieur Rossier looks at her reminds Ella of how he looks when he adds up the rent and the electricity, and all of a sudden she worries that he wants her to pay more.

"I have such happy memories of the house," Monsieur Rossier is saying. His expression has softened and Ella relaxes. "I lived there as a child, you know, with my parents. My mother had what I suppose is your room, although, of course, it was quite different then. She had all her furniture from when she was a young girl and it was like a salon." Ella cannot help picturing her bedroom transformed into a sort of storage room, crammed and crowded with antique furniture, blocking the windows and shutting out the light.

"Especially when she was older and could no longer come downstairs," Monsieur Rossier continues, "she stayed in her room and we would go up and visit her. It was always very pleasant and she was happy there. She died in that room, you know."

He is not trying to offend you, Ella admonishes herself. He is just an old man with old memories. Just listen and be still.

The maître d'hôtel comes around with the white mounds again, and Ella shakes her head. "*Non, merci,*" she tells him.

Monsieur Rossier takes another mound of rice, and Ella tries hard not to think of the havoc it will cause to his digestion. "Later, after my wife and I were married, we lived there with our two sons," Monsieur Rossier continues.

"Your son who lives in London—"

"Yes, two sons." Monsieur Rossier interrupts. "André who lives in London and another son, Yves. He was younger than André. A wonderful boy, handsome and full of spirit and lively. He was very popular with the people of the village. Everyone admired him and liked him. He loved to ride horses and to hunt, to play golf and tennis. My wife and I thought he could have become a professional athlete, but, of course, we did not want that for him. It was just an idea we had, you understand."

Ella takes a little more wine. Obviously, Yves was the prodigal son. Probably, he was arrogant and spoilt. She sympathizes with sensible and unathletic André and wants to resist Yves's facile charm.

Across the table, Monsieur Rossier is quiet. But then he rouses himself and says, "Life is strange, you know." He looks at Ella while the maître d'hôtel begins to clear the plates and replace them with clean ones. Ella smiles what she hopes is a kind, wise smile and she hopes that Monsieur Rossier will realize that she, too, understands about life and its strangeness. After all, isn't he aware that she must have been through a lot herself? Here she is alone in a foreign country with her small children. But she sees that he is no longer looking at her. He is playing with his fork.

Ella does not know what to say when Monsieur Rossier suddenly says, "Yves was killed." In an effort to show grief, she screws up her face—her mouth turned down, her eyes squinted. "I'm so sorry," she finally says as the maître d'hôtel nudges her elbow with a platter of *paupiettes de veau.* Surrounding the veal are small peas and little onions, the kind that look as if they came from a can, and Ella serves herself sparingly.

Monsieur Rossier helps himself to peas and onions, but no veal, and continues, "Yes, Yves was killed. No, not in the war, although he wanted very much to enlist with de Gaulle and the Free French. He was only fifteen at the time, and his mother and I were very much against it, of course. We forbade him. André was in the Resistance, and that was bad enough. God knows, we worried about him night and day."

Monsieur Rossier sighs deeply and takes a mouthful of peas and onions. "It was such a stupid accident, really. So unnecessary. He was on his way to Bordeaux to visit friends and spend the weekend. It was a house party. The plane service had just resumed, and flights were still very infrequent. In any case, the planes were small and I suppose old, and something went wrong with the landing gear. The pilot was not alerted. The plane crashed and burned. All the passengers and crew were killed and Yves was among them. They said they were all killed instantly."

Ella lowers her head so that he cannot see her face and busies herself cutting up the veal on her plate.

"They telephoned to tell us and it was already late and, of course, I shall never forget it. My wife and I were preparing to go upstairs to bed. We had been out that night, not far from here, to see friends, and we had just gotten home. We were living in Belle Fontaine, I remember it so well, and we had just begun work on the château. The telephone rang and I said to my wife, 'Good heavens, who could that be calling us at this hour?'

But I knew. And when I went to pick up the receiver, I knew what they were going to tell me. It was the police in Bordeaux."

Ella can picture it exactly. She can see Monsieur Rossier and his wife as they are about to go upstairs to the bedroom, and then she can see Monsieur Rossier hesitate and look inquiringly at his wife, before he goes to answer the phone, which is in the hallway right next to the landing of the stairs, not far, just a few steps away, but far enough for him to feel a premonition and be afraid.

Ella finishes her food slowly. Yes, the peas and onions are most certainly from a can. How strange, she thinks, remembering the large vegetable garden Monsieur Rossier cultivates in the summer. From her bedroom window, Ella had watched how the gardener worked all day among the neat rows of lettuce, spinach, onions and, no doubt, peas. She refuses a second helping.

"Who would guess that something like that would happen to us? We were so happy, so . . ."—Monsieur Rossier searches for a word—"so united. And life never seemed quite the same after that, for my wife and me."

Ella is reminded of the young Japanese woman and her child in the yellow slicker, and she tries to imagine how their lives have changed. She is tempted to say something about the recent plane crash—surely

Monsieur Rossier would remember it—but she decides not to.

"Yves would be a grown man by now, in his forties, with children of his own, like André. Still, I can't help thinking about it and how different things would perhaps be if he were alive. He would be living in Belle Fontaine, and he would be here tonight for dinner."

But I wouldn't be, Ella is tempted to say, but she knows perfectly well that she cannot, even for an instant, risk such a lighthearted comment. She is nothing to Monsieur Rossier and although, at the moment, she would like to try to be, she also knows that never, never, can she be of comfort to Monsieur Rossier.

"I always watch the Saturday night show on the television," Monsieur Rossier says as, obediently, Ella follows him back into the sitting room, where two straight-back chairs have been placed directly in front of the large brilliant television already turned on too loud. Pointing to one of the chairs, Monsieur Rossier excuses himself and leaves Ella alone in the room. The fire has nearly gone out and the room no longer feels cozy and warm. Ella wishes she could get a cigarette from her purse, but Monsieur Rossier, she guesses, would not approve of her smoking. The soufflé that she had looked forward to was a disappointment—it tasted of egg whites and vanilla extract. Looking over again at the photograph of the four grandsons, she idly wonders which of the four is Yves and whether he is like the uncle he was named after. Probably the opposite—studious and quiet—she decides. Overhead, she hears water running, then Monsieur Rossier's heavy step, on the stairs, and Ella wishes there was something she could do for him.

Monsieur Rossier turns off the light and settles into the chair next to her. The room now, except for the light from the television, is completely dark; Ella can just make out the outline of Monsieur Rossier's profile. It is a variety show and a young man wearing a frilly shirt and a medal around his neck is singing. It is hard for Ella to tell if Monsieur Rossier is enjoying the show—his profile seems alert enough.

There is a discreet knock, and the maître d'hôtel pushes open the door with a tray full of bottles and glasses—enough, Ella thinks, for twenty people. Putting the tray down on a table near their chairs, he bids them good night. "Help yourself," Monsieur Rossier tells Ella. "There's brandy, liqueur, fruit juices, everything, I think."

Why not? she thinks as she gets up from her chair and fumbles among the bottles and glasses in the dark. She finally takes a bottle that feels like a brandy bottle and pours herself almost a full glass. It is not brandy but a liqueur, a pear liqueur. The liqueur is very strong and tastes like fire going down her throat.

Sitting in the chair next to Monsieur Rossier, the glass in her hand, Ella tries to concentrate on the television but cannot, and she starts to think again about what she is doing here—in this foreign country, in this ugly château, on a Saturday night with an old man who is nothing to her and to whom she is nothing. She shivers. Hadn't Monsieur Rossier told her more than once how, in order to economize, the maître d'hôtel turned off the heat at night? Outside, it must be even colder. She should be in a city, in a brightly lit restaurant or a nightclub, warm and intimate, with a handsome young man who is holding her hand and with whom she is going to dance. The young man in the nightclub looks like one of Monsieur Rossier's grandsons. Again, Ella is reminded of Yves. Perhaps she would have liked him after all, perhaps even loved him, and who knows, they might have gotten married and it would not matter that he was so much older than Ella, he was so extraordinarily good-looking and athletic. He would have loved her back, too, and, of course, they would be living at Belle Fontaine, only it would be different. She would not be paying rent and she would feel close to this old man; she would be his daughter-in-law, and perhaps there would be children, his grandchildren. And life would be filled with excitement and pleasure, parties and trips, riding, tennis and skiing, and always handsome Yves at her side and in her bed. Ella imagines making love to Yves.

On the television, a tall woman in a long white dress has replaced the singer, and Monsieur Rossier leans forward in his chair to take a closer look at her. Monsieur Rossier, Ella has heard, was once one of the leading businessmen in France. He made a name for himself and a fortune as well. Actually, he had always had the name, for his family was an old and distinguished one, but when he took over the family business, he raised the name to a new and glorious height. Probably, he was ruthless and forced smaller companies out or bought them up. Probably, too, families went bankrupt or lost their fortunes as Monsieur Rossier cornered the market and became enormously rich. But he was quietly rich, discreetly rich. He did not own yachts and racehorses, or spend his free time in Monte Carlo gambling with movie stars. Mainly he owned land. He bought vast forests in the north of France, thousands of hectares, which he supervised himself and on which he grew fir trees that were sold to paper mills. He built the ugly château and he owned a large apartment in Paris in the Eighth Arrondissement, near the Étoile. In the winter, he took his family to Saint-Moritz to ski, where he had gone as a small boy with his own parents. They had gone in sleds, with trunks full of monogrammed linen and personal servants to look after them in the hotel; in the summer he and his family went to Deauville for the sea air. And he had been content, for he had always stood for what was decent and honest and never mind that some people had criticized him for being too severe and for being a bit heartless. He had a clear conscience. One had to have high standards; otherwise one never got anywhere. And had he not always worked hard for everything he got?

The dancer on the television is quite beautiful, Monsieur Rossier decides, but not as beautiful as his wife. Mostly, if he thinks about the years before Yves's death, he thinks about his wife and how they really did not spend enough time together, and he regrets it now. It seemed as if there was always something they had to do, someplace they had to be, a reception, a ball, a weekend. She, in particular, had liked the receptions. She liked to dress well and she had lovely clothes and, it is true, she looked beautiful in them. He thinks about how she looked in the long gowns with the jewelry he had given her and he feels sad. But he has had a good life—with a few exceptions, of course. Yves's death. The war, too, although that had its advantages for his business. Yes, he has had a good life and he cannot complain even if he can no longer eat properly and his bowels do not move, but all that is minor. After all, he will be ninety-three this year. And sometimes he feels lonely but not always. Tonight he has the tenant from Belle Fontaine sitting in the chair next to him. She is not bad looking for an American and she is polite. You never know about tenants, especially women, single women, and the children. He had been very worried at first that they would destroy his mother's old furniture. Children nowadays have no discipline, and there is no one but a fat Spanish girl to look after them, and each time he has gone to the house, the Spanish girl is sitting in the living room dressed in strange clothes and smoking and the children are nowhere to be seen. Surely, there is something she could be doing, but of course it isn't any of his business and the house is kept clean and orderly. There are flowers, and it looks almost the way it did when he and his wife lived there. And the maître d'hôtel tells him that as yet nothing has been broken and they are looking after his things, which shows that you can never tell about people. Perhaps, it will work out after all. She is really quite nice—not energetic enough perhaps, and too timid—but on the whole that is better than the other way around. The dancer on the television is pirouetting in her long white dress, and the music is familiar. He cannot remember right away what it is. . . . Oh, yes, he thinks, The Skaters' Waltz. *How many times has he waltzed to it with his wife.*

Ella also recognizes the waltz. When she was first married and before the children were born, she and her husband took ballroom lessons. They enjoyed dancing together and got fairly proficient at the fox-trot, the two-step, even the tango, but for some reason, they never quite mastered the waltz. She can still hear how her husband would groan out loud when they had to practice it—*one, two, three, one, two, three*—then, how, suddenly clumsy, he stepped on her feet and bumped her into the other couples. Unapologetic, he laughed and, as a joke, she remembers, he called her "Ginger." In the dark, sitting next to Monsieur Rossier, Ella smiles to herself at the memory. Abruptly, the music comes to an end and the screen changes color. A voice announces something else, a tumbling act.

The variety show finishes at eleven and they sit and watch the news. Monsieur Rossier falls asleep and snores during the report of the mine explosion in the Pas-de-Calais, the threat of strikes, the rain and cold forecast for the morrow. Ella has to touch his arm to wake him when it is over. Startled, Monsieur Rossier shakes himself, embarrassed; then, slowly he gets up to turn off the television. In the dark, Monsieur Rossier gropes for the switch by the door. When he finds it, the room is filled with bright, white light that makes Ella squint. She glances over at Monsieur Rossier, who is standing by the door, and he looks tired and ill. His face is gray and his eyes are hidden behind a film of water, age and grief. Ella walks past him to the hall, where her coat is neatly folded on a chair. She puts it on while Monsieur Rossier undoes the bolts on the front door and opens it for her.

She thanks him and says, "Good night."

Looking out past Ella into the night, Monsieur Rossier merely nods.

The cold air catches Ella as the door shuts behind her. She hardly dares breathe, and when she looks up at the sky, there are no stars. She turns back toward the château as it goes dark, and everything is suddenly black. She remembers the dog and prays that he is inside with the gatekeeper. But she is frightened of other things as well—nameless things—as, her heart pounding, she begins to run past the field. "Don't be a fool," she tells herself. "What can possibly happen to you?" and she makes herself slow down. In the distance, she can see a faint light coming from the drawing room window in the house.

The telephone is ringing when she opens the door to Belle Fontaine. It is very late and she cannot imagine who might be calling her at this hour. For a few seconds, she stands there in the hallway right by the stairs that lead up to her bedroom, unable to move and also, in the same spot where, so many years ago, Monsieur Rossier stood. *The children,* Ella thinks, then, *an accident.* In spite of herself, she pictures the plane going down. The phone continues to ring and, still a little out of breath from hurrying in the cold, she finally picks up the receiver. It takes her a moment to recognize Monsieur Rossier's voice. "Yes, thank you, I'm home," Ella tells him, relieved, but immediately she remembers how duped she had felt when she discovered that the person on the television in the long white dress dancing to *The Skaters' Waltz* was a man and not a woman. A man impersonating a woman. Not sure whether Monsieur Rossier had realized that, Ella had started to tell him but changed her mind.

Ice

On board the *Caledonia Star*, sailing through the Beagle Channel and past the city of Ushuaia on the way to Antarctica, Maud's husband says, "Those lights will probably be the last we'll see for a while."

Mountains rise stark and desolate on both sides of the channel; already there does not look to be room for people. Above, the evening sky, a sleety gray, shifts to show a little patch of the lightest blue. Standing on deck next to her husband, Maud takes it for a good omen— the ship will not founder, they will not get seasick, they will survive the journey, their marriage more or less still intact.

Also, Maud spots her first whale, another omen; she spots two.

*   *   *

In the morning, early, the ship's siren sounds a fire drill. Maud and Peter quickly put on waterproof pants, boots, sweaters, parkas, hats, gloves—in the event of an emergency, they have been told to wear their warmest clothes. They strap on the life jackets that are hanging from a hook on the back of their cabin door and follow their fellow passengers up the stairs. The first officer directs them to the ship's saloon; they are at Station 2, he tells them. On deck, Maud can see the lifeboats being lowered smoothly and efficiently and not, Maud can't help but think, how it must have been on board the *Andrea Doria*—a woman who survived the ship's collision once told Maud how undisciplined and negligent the Italian crew was. The first officer is French—the captain and most of the other officers are Norwegian—and he is darkly handsome. As he explains the drill, he looks steadily and impassively above the passengers' heads as if, Maud thinks, the passengers are cattle; in vain, she tries to catch his eye. When one of the passengers tries to interrupt with a joke, the first officer rebukes him with a sharp shake of the head and continues speaking.

When the drill is over and still wearing his life jacket, Peter leaves the saloon, saying he is going up on deck to breathe some fresh air, and Maud goes back down to the cabin.

*   *   *

Of the eighty or so passengers on board the *Caledo-nia Star*, the majority are couples; a few single women travel together; one woman is in a wheelchair. The average age, Maud guesses, is mid- to late sixties and, like them—Peter was a lawyer and Maud a speech therapist (she still works three days a week at a private school)—most are retired professionals. And although Maud and Peter learned about the cruise from their college alumni magazine, none of the passengers—some of whom they assume must have attended the same college—look familiar to them. "Maybe they all took correspondence courses," Peter says. Since his retirement, Peter has been restless and morose. "No one," he complains to Maud, "answers my phone calls anymore." The trip to Antarctica was Maud's idea.

When Maud steps out on deck to look for Peter, she does not see him right away. The ship rolls from side to side—they have started to cross the Drake Passage—and already they have lost sight of land. When Maud finally finds Peter, her relief is so intense she nearly shouts as she hurries over to him. Standing at the ship's rail, looking down at the water, Peter does not appear to notice Maud. Finally, without moving his head, he says in a British-inflected, slightly nasal voice, "Did you know that

the Drake Passage is a major component of the coupled
ocean-atmosphere climate system and that it connects
all the other major oceans and that it influences the
water-mass characteristics of the deep water over a large
portion of the world?"

"Of course, darling," Maud answers in the same sort
of voice and takes Peter's arm. "Everyone knows that."

Peter has an almost photographic memory and is,
Maud likes to say, the smartest man she has ever met.
Instead of being a lawyer, Peter claims that he would
have preferred being a mathematician. He is an attrac-
tive man; tall and athletic-looking, although he walks
with a slight limp—he broke his leg as a child and the
bones did not set properly—which gives him a certain
vulnerability and adds to his appeal (privately, Maud ac-
cuses him of exaggerating the limp to elicit sympathy).
And he still has a full head of hair, notwithstanding that
it has turned gray, which he wears surprisingly long.
Maud, too, is good-looking; slim, tall and blonde (the
blonde is no longer natural but such a constant Maud
would be hard put to say what her natural color is); her
blue eyes, she claims, are still her best feature. Together,
they make a handsome couple; they have been married
for over forty years.

Maud knows Peter so well that she also knows that
when he adopts this bantering tone with her either he

is hiding something or he is feeling depressed. Or both. Instinctively, she tightens her grip on his arm.

"Let's go in," she says to him in her normal voice, "I'm cold."

In their cabin, the books, the clock, the bottle of sleeping pills, everything that had been neatly stacked on the nightstand is, on account of the ship's motion, lying pell-mell on the floor.

Instead of a double bed, their cabin has two narrow bunks, placed side by side. The bunks are made up in an unusual way, a Norwegian way, Maud guesses—the sheet wrapped around the blanket as if it were a parcel and tucked in. In her bed, Maud feels as if she were lying inside a cocoon; also, she does not dislike sleeping alone for a change. As if Peter could read her mind—he has an uncanny ability to do this sometimes—he pats the side of his bunk and says, "Come here for a minute, Maud." Maud hesitates, then decides not to answer. She does not feel like making love—too much trouble and often, recently, sex does not work out, which makes her anxious and Peter anxious and angry both. Over their heads, on the wall, the public-address speaker crackles and a voice says: "Long before the poet Samuel Coleridge penned his *Rime of the Ancient Mariner,* the albatross was a creature of reverence and superstition. The sailors believed that when their captain died, his soul took the form of an albatross. Of course I cannot speak for our excellent Captain Halvorsen, but I, for one, would not mind being reincarnated as an albatross." In the bed next to Maud, Peter snorts and says again, "Maudie, come over here." Maud pretends not to hear him. "By the way, my name is Michael," the voice continues, "and in case you have not yet met me I am your naturalist on board." Peter says something that Maud does not quite catch although she can guess at the meaning. "The albatross has the largest wingspan—the record, I believe is thirteen feet, three inches—and the oldest known albatross is seventy years old. When he is ten, the albatross goes back to where he was born to mate—" Maud tenses for a comment from Peter but this time he makes none. The public-address speaker crackles with static: ". . . feeds at night . . . eats luminous squid, fish and krill." Maud looks over at Peter's bunk and sees that Peter's eyes are closed. Relieved, she reaches up to turn down the volume on the speaker as Michael says, "The albatross will fly for miles without moving its wings, or setting foot on land. Soaring and gliding over the water, the albatross's zigzag flight is determined by the wind."

*   *   *

The captain's cocktail party is held in the saloon—or, as Maud refers to it, Emergency Station 2. She is dressed in her best slacks and a red cashmere sweater, and Peter wears his blue blazer and a tie. The saloon is packed tight with passengers who are all talking at once. Right away, Maud orders a vodka martini at the bar while Peter has a beer.

"Take it easy," Peter says, handing her the martini.

The ship's motion is more pronounced and Maud hangs on to the edge of the bar with one hand and holds her martini glass in the other. Sometimes Maud drinks too much. She blames her age and the fact that she is thin and cannot hold her liquor the way she used to—not the actual amount she drinks. Standing in the center of the room, Captain Halvorsen is a tall man with thinning red hair; he smiles politely as he talks to the passengers. Maud guesses that he must dread this evening and the enforced sociability. Looking around the room, she does not see the darkly handsome first officer. A woman holding a golf club—which, at first, Maud thinks is a cane— walks over to them and, standing next to Peter at the bar, orders a glass of white wine.

"If I am not mistaken, that's a five iron you have in your hand," Peter says to her in his nasal voice.

"Yes, it is," the woman answers. She is dark and trim and does not smile.

"Do you always travel with a golf club?" Peter, when he wants, can be charming and he can act as if he is completely entranced by what the person he is speaking to is saying. If that person happens to be a woman, Maud tends to resent it, even though she knows that Peter's attention may not be entirely genuine. Peter continues, "By the way, my name is Peter and this is my wife, Maud."

"I'm Barbara," the woman says. "And, yes, I always travel with my golf club."

"As protection?" Maud manages to ask.

"No," Barbara frowns. "My goal is to drive a golf ball in every country of the world."

"Oh."

"And have you?" Peter asks. He does a little imitation golf swing, holding his bottle of beer in both hands. When, in the past, Maud has accused Peter of toying with people, Peter has accused Maud of misreading him.

"As a matter of fact, I have. Or nearly. Except for Antarctica, which of course is not a country but a continent, and a few African nations, which are too dangerous. I began twenty years ago—"

Why? Maud is tempted to ask.

"After my husband died," Barbara says as if to answer Maud.

"Can you get me another martini?" Maud asks Peter.

* * *

That night, Maud cannot sleep. Every time she closes her eyes, she feels dizzy and nauseated and she has to open her eyes again; she tries sitting up in bed. To make matters worse, the *Caledonia Star* creaks and shudders as all night it pitches and lurches through a heavy sea. Once, after a particularly violent lurch, Maud calls out to Peter but either he is asleep and does not hear her or, perverse, he does not answer her. To herself, Maud vows that she will never have another drink.

In the morning, at seven according to the clock that is on the floor—Maud has finally managed to sleep for a few hours—Maud and Peter are awoken by the now familiar voice on the public-address speaker.

"Good morning, folks! It's Michael! I hope you folks were not still sleeping! For those of you who are on the starboard side of the ship—that means the right side for the landlubbers—if you look out your porthole real quick, you'll see a couple of minke whales."

When Maud looks outside, the sea is calm and it is raining.

"Do you see them?" Peter asks from his bed.

"No," Maud says. "I don't see any minke whales."

"Michael is lying to us," Peter says, rolling over on

to his other side. "Be a good girl and give me a back rub. This mattress is for the birds."

In the rubber Zodiac, Maud starts to feel better. The cold air clears her head and she is looking forward to walking on land. Behind her, the *Caledonia Star* rests solidly at anchor as they make their way across to Livingston Island. The passengers in the boat are all wearing orange life jackets as well as identical red parkas—parkas they were obliged to purchase prior to setting sail. When Maud had inquired about the parkas, she was told that red was easy to see and made it easier for the crew to tell whether any passenger was left behind on shore. And had a passenger ever been left behind? Maud continued to ask. Yes, once. A woman had tried to hide. Hide? Why? Maud had asked again, but she got no reply.

Holding her golf club between her legs, Barbara sits across from them in the Zodiac. Instead of a cap she wears a visor that has Golfers Make Better Lovers printed on it. Michael, the naturalist, is young, blond and bearded, and he drives the Zodiac with smooth expertise. Once he lands the boat, he gives each passenger a hand, cautioning them: "Careful where you walk, the ground may be slippery. And, steer clear of those seals," he also says, pointing. "Especially the big fur seal, he's not friendly."

Looking like giant rubber erasers, about a dozen seals are lying close together along the shore; their beige and gray hides are mottled and scarred. Except for one seal who raises his head to look at them as they walk past—the fur seal, no doubt—none of the seals move. Maud gives them a wide berth and makes no eye contact; Peter, on the other hand, deliberately walks up closer to the seals and takes several photos of them.

A few yards inland, Maud sees Barbara lean over to tee up a golf ball. She watches as Barbara takes up her stance and takes a few practice swings. Several of the other passengers are watching her as well. One man calls out, "Make it a hole in one, Barbara!" The golf ball sails straight toward the brown cliffs that rise from the shore; a few people applaud. Barbara tees up and hits another golf ball, then another. Each time, the sound is a sharp crack, like ice breaking.

Michael is right, it is slippery. Wet shale and bits of snow litter the ground; also there are hundreds— no, perhaps, thousands—of penguins on Livingston Island. Maud has to watch where she steps. It would not do, she thinks, to break a leg in Antarctica or to crush a penguin. Like the seals, the penguins appear to be oblivious of people. They are small and everywhere underfoot and Maud feels as if she is walking among dwarves.

When Peter catches up to her, he says, "You think one of these penguins is going to try to brood on a golf ball."

"Incubate, you mean," Maud says. "You brood on a chick."

"Whatever," Peter answers, turning away from her. He does not like being corrected, and although Maud should know better by now, old habits die hard.

In the Zodiac, on the way back to the *Caledonia Star*, the wind has picked up and the sea is rougher. In spite of Michael's efforts, waves slap at the boat's sides and cold spray wets the backs of the passengers' red parkas.

"Tomorrow, we will see icebergs," Captain Halvorsen promises during dinner. Maud and Peter are sitting at his table along with another couple, Bryan and Janet. Bryan claims to have been in the same college class as Peter and to remember him well (he alludes to an incident involving the misuse of cafeteria trays, but Peter has no recollection of it and shakes his head). Janet, a tall brunette with smooth olive skin and dark full eyebrows, is much younger; she never attended college, she tells Maud, giggling. She took up modeling instead.

"If the ice were to melt," Captain Halvorsen tells Peter, "the water would rise sixty-six meters."

"Isn't a meter like a yard?" Janet asks. "I was never any good at math."

Sitting next to Maud, Bryan, who is in real estate, is describing the booming building industry in Florida, where he lives.

"The grounding line is where the ice mass begins to float," Maud overhears Captain Halvorsen say. "In Antarctica, icebergs form when ice breaks away from large flat plates called ice shelves."

"I read that the Ross Ice Shelf is the size of the state of Connecticut," Peter says.

"The size of France," Captain Halvorsen says.

Leaning over, Janet says something to Peter that Maud cannot hear, which makes him laugh. Maud watches, as still laughing, Peter puts his hand on Janet's forearm and pats it in a gesture of easy camaraderie.

"Can you pass the wine, Bryan?" Maud interrupts him.

"Eighty-five percent of the ice in the world is in Antarctica," Captain Halvorsen says. Then, as a sort of afterthought, he adds, "And six percent of the ice in the world is in Greenland."

And the rest? The nine percent? Maud wishes to ask but does not.

* * *

For years, as a child, Maud had a recurring dream. A nightmare. In her sleep, she always knew when the nightmare was beginning but she was unable to stop it or wake herself up. The other thing, too, was that Maud could never describe it. The dream had nothing to do with people or monsters or violent situations or anything she might know or recognize. The dream could not be put into words. The closest way she could come to describing it was to say that it was about numbers (even so, that was not quite right, as the numbers were not the familiar ones like 8 or 17 or 224); they were something other. (When consulted about the nightmare, the family physician suggested that Maud stop taking math for a while but, at school, math was Maud's best subject.) The numbers (if in fact they were numbers) in the dream always started out small and manageable—although, again, Maud knew that was temporary, for soon they multiplied and became so large and unmanageable and incomprehensible that Maud was swept away into a kind of terrible abyss, a kind of black hole full of numbers.

It has been years now since Maud has thought about the dream. Antarctica, the vastness, the ice, the inhospitable landscape, is what she assumes has reminded her of it. When she tries to describe the dream to Peter and mentions the math part, Peter says he knows just what she means.

"You're in good company, all sorts of people had it. The Greeks, Aristotle, Archimedes, Pascal."

"The dream?"

"No, what the dream stands for."

"Which is?" Maud is not sure whether Peter is being serious.

"The terror of the infinite.

"Interestingly, the ancient Greeks did not include zero or infinity in their mathematics," Peter continues, displaying his fondness for the arcane. "Their word for *infinity* was also their word for *mess*."

Captain Halvorsen is right. The next morning, they see icebergs. The sea is filled with them. Icebergs of all shapes and sizes. Some are as tall as six-story buildings, others remind Maud of modern sculptures and are tinged with blue—a brilliant aquamarine blue. It is also snowing.

Despite the snow, Peter spends the morning on deck with his camera, taking pictures. When Maud joins him, he tells her, "Have you ever seen anything like those icebergs? Have you ever seen a blue like that?"

"Are you warm enough?" Maud asks. A part of her—a part she dislikes—resents seeing Peter so happy and excited about the icebergs, and she feels excluded.

At the same time, she also envies his ability to be so genuinely absorbed and enchanted by nature—at home, Peter is always pointing out large, beautiful trees to her. His appreciation seems pure and unmotivated and Maud wishes she could share it but she is too self-conscious. Too self-referential, she decides. She cannot look at the stars without wishing for a falling one, or gaze at the sea without thinking "drown."

Each time the *Caledonia Star* runs into a large ice floe, there is a loud thumping noise, but since the ship's hull is made out of steel, there is no need for concern. Many of the ice floes have penguins and seals on them. When the ship goes by, alarmed, the penguins dive off like bullets; the seals, indifferent, do not move. Often, blood, looking like paint splashed on a canvas, stains the ice around the seals—the remains of their kill. In addition to fur seals, Maud is told, there are crabeater seals, Ross seals, leopard seals, elephant seals and Weddell seals.

"A marine mammal exhales before he dives," Michael is saying over the public-address speaker, "and oxygen is stored in his blood, not in his lungs."

This time, Maud and Peter are making love on one of the bunks.

"Shall I turn him off?" Maud starts to move away.

"No. Stay put." Peter has an erection.

"Seals collapse their lungs when they dive. Their heart rate drops and their arteries constrict. In fact, everything is shut down—"

Maud half-listens.

"Except for the brain, the adrenal and the placenta —that is, of course, if the seal is pregnant—"

Afterward, still lying pressed together on the little bunk, Maud frees her arm, which has gone to sleep, from under Peter and, as if to make up for her movement, which breaks the postcoital spell, she kisses Peter lightly. Also, in spite of herself, she asks, "So what are you going to do with all the photographs you took of icebergs?"

Peter does not answer Maud right away. He shifts his body away from her a little before he says in the British-inflected, nasal voice, "Why, enlarge them, naturally."

Instead of going ashore again in the Zodiac with the others, Maud decides to remain on board. Except for the woman in the wheelchair, who appears to be asleep (her eyes are closed and she breathes heavily), Maud is alone in the saloon and, from where she is sitting reading, or trying to read, her book, she can watch the passengers, dressed in their red parkas, disembark at Fort Lockroy, the British station. She watches as they spread out and start to climb the snow-covered hill behind the station. Some of the passengers have brought along ski poles and Maud tries to pick out which red parka belongs to Peter and which belongs to Janet, but the figures are too far away. She thinks again about the woman who tried to hide and again she wonders why. Was the woman suicidal? But freezing to death, Maud also thinks, may not be such a bad way to die. How did the Emily Dickinson poem go? "As Freezing persons, recollect the Snow— / First—Chill—then Stupor—then the letting go—." In spite of herself, Maud shivers. Then she makes herself open her book. When next she looks up, all the figures in their red parkas have disappeared.

"You didn't miss anything," Peter tells Maud when he returns from the station. Nevertheless, he looks animated. "There was a museum, which was kind of creepy—an old sled and some frying pans—but Janet bought some postcards."

"Ah, lovely Janet," Maud says.

"What do you mean by that?" Peter asks.

"What do you suppose I mean?"

"For god's sake, Maud, why must you always be suspicious of me? Why do you always attribute some underhand motive to everything I do?" Peter says, before he turns and limps out of the saloon, leaving Maud.

The woman in the wheelchair has woken up; she gives a little embarrassed cough.

The first time, twenty or so years ago, Maud accused Peter of having an affair, the discussion had turned violent—Maud threw a plate of food at Peter and Peter picked up a glass full of wine and flung it across the table at Maud, shouting, "I can't live like this!" Then he left home for three days. When finally he returned, he did not say where he had been and Maud did not ask. What Maud remembers vividly is her panic. During the time Peter was gone, she could hardly breathe, let alone eat, and she could not sleep. She was assailed by all kinds of conflicting emotions, but the dominant one was fear: the fear that she had driven Peter to some action she would regret and the fear that she would never see him again.

When the *Caledonia Star* crosses the Antarctic Circle, all the passengers crowd on to the bridge to look. The sky is a cloudless blue and the sea calm but the horizon is a wall of icebergs. Maud recognizes the handsome French first officer up in the crow's nest, dressed in a bright yellow slicker and waterproof pants. He is reporting back to Captain Halvorsen on the bridge by walkie-talkie. The ship's chief officer is tracing the ship's course on a sea chart with a compass and a protractor; on the radar screen, the larger tabular icebergs show up as small luminous points.

Below on deck, Peter is looking through his binoculars.

"What do you see?" Maud asks but she cannot hear his answer.

By then, Maud is able to recognize most of the passengers on board the ship, and she knows many of them by name. One flight below their cabin, she has discovered the gym and she exercises regularly on the treadmill. She has also become more tolerant—even of Barbara, the golfer—and has made a few friends. One is the woman in the wheelchair.

"She's from Philadelphia and she's already identified five different species of albatross," Maud tells Peter, "the gray-headed albatross, the sooty albatross, the wandering—"

"What's wrong with her?" Peter wants to know. "Why is she in a wheelchair?"

Maud shrugs. "I didn't ask."

After dinner one night, a film is shown in the saloon. The film is old and grainy and tells the true story of the perilous voyage of a ship named the *Peking*. Sailing around the Cape Horn, the *Peking* encounters a terrible storm—the mast breaks, waves crash on deck—and, to make matters worse, the captain of the *Peking* has brought his dog, a vicious little terrier, on board. The terrier is seen jumping up and biting the sailors who have as yet not been swept overboard. The dog provides a kind of gruesome comic relief and makes everyone laugh, including Maud and Peter.

When the film ends, Janet tells Maud, "I once had a dog who looked just like that. His name was Pepe."

"I love dogs," expansive, Maud answers her.

Peter moves to sit next to Janet and starts to describe a cruise he once took in the Mediterranean as a college student. "I was on deck one night after dinner —we were docked in Cannes—and my wallet, which was in my back pocket, must have fallen overboard—"

Maud has heard the story a thousand times and does not listen. Instead she strikes up a conversation with the woman in the wheelchair. "Have you always loved birds?" Maud asks.

"You can't imagine! The most extraordinary piece of luck," Peter is telling Janet as he leans in closer to her, "A fisherman caught my wallet in his net. The wallet had over a thousand dollars in cash in it—I was planning to buy a car in England, an MG—"

Looking over, Maud sees that Janet has stopped paying attention to what Peter is saying. She is looking past him toward the door of the saloon and Maud follows her gaze. She sees the handsome French first officer standing there; she sees him signal to Janet.

"Excuse me," Janet says, getting up and leaving the saloon.

"Pinned up on the wall of the Cannes police station was every last dollar . . ." Peter's voice trails off.

Maud looks away. She is fairly used to seeing Peter flirt but she is not used to seeing him defeated.

A few minutes later, Peter says, "I'm tired, I'm going to bed."

Maud would like to say something that might be of comfort to him but cannot think what that might be. She merely nods.

When Maud wakes up during the night to go to the bathroom (or *head*, as she knows she is supposed to call it), she sees that Peter is not in his bed. The sheets and blankets are half lying on the floor, as if Peter had thrown them off in a rush.

"Peter," Maud calls out in the dark.

Turning on the light, Maud goes to the bathroom, then quickly pulls her jeans over her nightgown, grabs her parka, a hat and gloves.

The ship's corridor is dimly lit and empty. As Maud half-runs toward the stairs, her steps echo eerily. All the cabin doors are shut and, briefly, she imagines the occupants sleeping peacefully inside. The ship's motor hums smoothly, there is an occasional thud of the hull hitting an ice floe. Her heart banging in her chest, Maud runs up to the saloon. The saloon, too, is dimly lit and empty. In the dining room, the chairs are stacked, the floor ready for cleaning. From there, she opens a door and goes out on deck. The cold air momentarily takes her breath away but the sky is unnaturally light. The ship's huge searchlights move back and forth over the sea, restlessly illuminating here an ice floe, there an iceberg. Inside the bridge house, Captain Halvorsen, holding a mug of coffee, stands next to the pilot at the wheel. The handsome first officer briefly glances up from the radar screen as Maud comes in.

"My husband—" she says.

"Is he ill?" Without taking his eyes from the horizon, Captain Halvorsen asks. "Has something happened?"

"I'm looking for him," Maud answers, intimidated.

His face expressionless, the first officer continues to study the radar screen.

Every few seconds the pilot at the wheel shouts out numbers, coordinates, compass points. He, too, pays Maud no attention.

Directly in front of the ship's bow, a tabular iceberg that is taller and longer than the *Caledonia Star* appears yellowish green in the spotlight. In the bridge house all the attention is fixed on getting safely past it and not on anything that Maud says or does. For a moment longer, Maud stands motionless, not daring to speak or breathe, and watches the boat's slow, safe progress past the iceberg.

"Where were you?" Peter asks when Maud opens the cabin door and switches on the light. He is in bed, the sheet and blanket neatly tucked in around him.

"Where were *you*?" Despite the enormous relief she feels on seeing him, Maud is angry.

Peter tells her he went up on deck for a few minutes and they must have missed each other. At night, he says, the icebergs look even more amazing. "All that uninhabitable empty space. So pure, so absolute." Peter sounds euphoric, then, as if suddenly remembering something important, he says, "Maud, it's four thirty in the morning."

Maud does not feel tired, nor does she feel any desire to sleep. Back in bed, she has switched off the light when Peter calls over to her, in his slightly inflected British voice, "Sweet dreams, darling."

Maud says nothing.

Lucky

The sound of cries from the cottage next door drift across the lawn to where Helen is sitting on her deck painting a picture and it takes her a moment to recognize what they are. A woman having an orgasm. The young tenant's girlfriend, she thinks. It is a Sunday in June and the only other sound Helen hears is the twittering of the barn swallows who, miraculously—or so it seems to Helen—have returned all the way to Long Island from Peru or from somewhere in South America to the very same nest they built last year, which is right over the door leading from the house to Helen's deck, and are now noisily occupied feeding their young. The tenant, a carpenter, is named Craig and he is tall and has curly red hair and Helen knows little about him except that, so far—he has been renting the cottage only since March—he has been a good tenant. He has paid his rent on time and has not yet given Helen cause for complaint by playing loud music or by blocking her parking spot with his white truck. Quite the contrary, she has found Craig helpful: he offered to take down the storm windows, and when, in May, Helen went to Tuscany for a week, Craig picked up her mail and kept an eye on things. Now, in spite of herself, Helen cannot help but wonder how Craig is making the woman come.

Helen starts to collect her easel and her paints in order to move indoors but then she remembers the barn swallows. She does not want to disturb them by opening and shutting the door while they are feeding their young. Five baby chicks were hatched two weeks ago and Helen has watched their progress almost obsessively—a part of her wishes she had installed the video camera she had read about on the Internet that was fitted with infrared lighting so she could watch the nesting activity—but she has made every effort not to upset the birds by her presence. She has kept her cat inside the house and away from them, and, except for placing a few sheets of newspaper under the nest, she has also refrained from cleaning up the birds' mess. Already Helen can tell, by the way the chicks lift their heads and open wide their bright yellow beaks and how much more aggressively demanding they are for their food, that soon they will be ready to fledge. Picking up her brush, Helen sits down again in front of her easel. She had been copying a picture postcard she bought in Tuscany of a painting by Ghirlandaio before she was interrupted. Mostly, she knows that she is afraid to step down onto the lawn and circle her house to go to the front door in case, in addition to hearing the woman's cries, she catches a glimpse through an open cottage window of naked, young bodies coupling.

Helen is no longer young, neither is she so old—and hasn't she heard tell how one always feels at least ten years younger than one actually is?—which would make her feel in her midforties. In Tuscany, Helen felt even younger. Something to do with the air, the wine at lunch, the light. She could have walked the streets of Lucca, Siena, San Gimignano—her favorite of the three towns—forever, there was so much to see, to do. In addition, she had experienced a feeling of freedom that she does not often feel at home, where she worries too much about the lawn, the plumbing, roof repairs. On the way back in the plane, Helen had promised herself that from now on she would travel more and go to places like Machu Picchu, Angkor Wat, Luang Prabang. She would be more adventurous.

All appears to be quiet again—no more sounds are coming from the cottage and the barn swallows have left to find more insects to feed their young—and Helen is

at last able to go indoors. A few minutes later, she hears
Craig's truck drive away and when she goes to the front
window to look, she sees the back of a woman's dark
head resting against Craig's.

"What's she like, anyway?" Gina asks.

"Who?"

Gina does not have to be at work until the afternoon
and they are driving to the beach, which, this month, is
still relatively uncrowded. Too cold yet to swim, they are
just going to walk. The truck windows are open and Craig
breathes deeply—he likes the smell of freshly mown
grass. Most of the houses he drives by are large and
expensive and are surrounded by well-trimmed privet
hedges, the gardens he can see are filled with lush hy-
drangea bushes and are manicured down to what he
calls a "fare-thee-well."

"Your landlady. How old do you suppose she is? I
bet I know why she rented you the cottage." Gina laughs
and rolls her dark eyes. She has a wide mouth and very
small teeth—they almost look like her baby teeth—her
only flaw. Last fall, she enrolled in law school and she
plans to do environmental law so that, among other
things, she can protect the wildlife on the island and
keep the dunes from further eroding on the beach. Gina

prides herself on her boldness and the boldness is what first attracted Craig, but now it tires him a little. "Seriously, she doesn't look half bad for her age."

"You just said you didn't know how old she was." For some reason, Craig feels protective of Helen, whom he hardly knows. The two of them, he thinks, have probably exchanged no more than a hundred words in the three months he has rented the cottage. And, if truth be told, he has not given her or the life she leads much thought except for the one morning when he was leaving for work early and he saw a young man in boxer shorts and a T-shirt standing in the kitchen with his back to the window and holding his cup out to Helen to fill. The young man's presence had surprised Craig but later she had said something to him about her son who had come to visit.

"She has grown-up kids, doesn't she?" Gina asks, as if she could read his mind.

Craig nods. Although he likes his work as a carpenter well enough, his secret ambition—not so secret, perhaps, since he has told Gina—is to save enough money to buy a boat, a sailboat, and sail for a year or two: sail across the Atlantic with a girl who is not afraid, a girl like Gina, maybe. "So far she hasn't hassled me about anything," he says.

"She paints—paints pictures," Craig also tells Gina, as if to vindicate Helen in Gina's eyes.

"She must be rich," Gina answers.

Up ahead on the road, Craig sees the flashing blue light of a police car and he slows down. A red BMW has gone off the road, leaving deep tire tracks in the grass. The car has hit a tree. The hood is completely smashed and the windshield is splintered into thousands of shards. The front door of the car on the driver's side has folded up at an odd angle and black smoke is coming out of the hood.

"Oh, my god," Gina says.

A policewoman, her hands on her hips, is standing next to the car. A policeman is sitting in the car talking on the radio.

Craig opens the door of the truck. "Stay there," he tells Gina, but she too is getting out.

"Turn off the ignition," Craig calls out to the policewoman.

"The door," policewoman yells back, as she starts to go around to the passenger side of the car.

"I'll get a fire extinguisher—I have one in my truck," Craig says, as he starts to go back.

Behind him, Craig can hear the wail of an ambulance. The wail is getting louder. Also, the siren of another police car.

By the time Craig has freed the fire extinguisher from where it was wedged under his seat, a second police

car and the ambulance have arrived. Craig watches as the
two paramedics carry a stretcher to the wrecked car; the
smoke from the hood, he notices with relief, has dwin-
dled to a thin wisp. From the way the paramedics move,
Craig sees that they are having trouble getting the driver
out of the car. When finally they do, the man—Craig can
tell by the trousers and shirt that it is a man—is having
convulsions; his body doubles up then straightens out
again in rapid succession, and the paramedics have to
strap him down tightly so that he does not fall off the
stretcher onto the ground.

"Let's go," Craig says to Gina, who is standing next
to him. He takes her arm and also says, "I wonder if he
is going to make it."

A long time ago when he was first learning how to
drive, Craig ran over the neighbor's cat. It was not his
fault—the cat had darted out on the road and Craig did
not have time to stop the car. When he got out—Craig
had run over the cat's back—the cat was convulsing,
arching and straightening its body just like the man,
and Craig, to put the cat out of its misery, had gotten
back into the car, shifted into reverse and run over it
again.

"He must have been going like hell," Craig says
once he is back in the truck.

In the seat next to him, Gina bursts into tears.

*   *   *

Helen has been married three times: once widowed and twice divorced—how did the rhyme about Henry VIII and his six wives go? *Divorced, beheaded, died, divorced, beheaded, survived.* Somehow, she feels as if she, too, has survived—only just. Her first husband, Raymond, decided, after they had two children and had been married fifteen years, that he was gay and left her for a man. Raymond and the man, a Cuban, live in a condo in South Beach, Florida; the children keep in touch and visit him and Javier there. Her second husband died less than a year after they were married; he had a heart attack in the street, outside his office on Wall Street. Alec, her third husband, is an alcoholic and a liar. He can also be very charming. The last time Helen saw him, about four months ago, she was on her way to the city and they happened to take the same bus. They rode in together. He told her then how he was on the wagon and had been sober for nearly a year, but she had known better than to believe him. He also said how he was on his way to an exhibition at the Whitney and she remembers that he said something that made her laugh—only she cannot remember what exactly—about how dreadful modern art was maybe. Helen met Alec in a life class she had signed up for. He was the teacher.

Back out on her deck, Helen is transplanting herbs into pots: basil, rosemary, thyme and nasturtiums, the latter for a little color, and she likes to add the edible orange flower to salad. She is vaguely aware of the barn swallows flying to and fro over her head to their nest. Inside the house, the phone starts to ring and, looking up, Helen listens while the machine picks up.

"Helen, are you there?" She hears a woman's voice saying. "It's Daphne, Alec's sister. I'm calling you from Pennsylvania. Alec has been in an accident. Can you call me back, please? My number here—"

"Not again," Helen says to herself. Twice, while she was married to him, Alec had been involved in car accidents. The first time he broke his nose and wrist; the second time he was driving Helen's new car and totaled it, but he himself did not suffer a single scratch. The woman who was with him however—Alec claimed that he hardly knew her, he was just giving her a lift home from work—was killed. Killed instantly. At the trial later, Alec swore that he had fallen asleep at the wheel—he was tired, not drunk—and the woman's death was judged an accident and Alec was lucky. He was acquitted of all charges, including driving under the influence. Shaking her head—Alec, she thinks, is the sort of person who always manages to land on his feet—Helen goes back to digging a hole in the soil for the basil plant she is holding in her hand. She cannot now remember what the woman's name was, the woman killed in the accident, only that it was an unusual name.

In the car, Helen tries to think about something else, something pleasant. She thinks about Tuscany and the good time she had there. Everyone, she recalls, was so cheerful, like the porter and the maid at the hotel where she stayed: *Sta bene, signora?* The maid kept asking her with a smile. *Sì, grazie,* Helen had mustered her few words of Italian to reply. Also, she had particularly liked another couple on the tour; they were from Vermont. They promised to stay in touch. Ah, and the food! She ate like a horse and did not gain a single pound! Helen turns down the street that leads to the hospital.

When Helen had finally called back, Daphne said that Alec was in intensive care. "They don't think he is going to make it. I could tell by the way the doctor spoke," Daphne said.

"You know Alec. He always makes it," Helen told Daphne.

"But I'll go, of course," she also said.

After hanging up the phone, she had sat for a moment longer stroking the cat who was sitting on her lap. When she and Alec said good-bye to each other on the bus after they reached town, Alec said to her, "Let's have lunch together some time" and Helen, defensive, answered, "Sure. When do you suggest? How about never?" Now, she regrets her attempt at sarcasm and wishes that they had met for lunch and for perhaps more, but Alec, always good-natured, laughed at her remark and waved before disappearing in the crowd on the street.

"Are you a relative?" the nurse at the desk asks Helen.

Helen starts to shake her head then changes her mind. "His wife," she lies—after all, she once was and she has kept his name.

"Please sit down," the nurse tells Helen in a kinder tone. "A doctor will be with you shortly."

The badge on the doctor's white coat says Dr. Harris-Mehta and she is blonde and petite and young enough to be Helen's daughter.

"Your husband, Mrs. ah . . ."

"Mallory."

"Yes, sorry—Mrs. Mallory—Mr. Mallory did not suffer," Dr. Harris-Mehta starts to tell Helen. "Mr. Mallory had a severed aorta, his thoracic artery . . . ," she pauses, "as well as massive trauma to the head. He was not conscious."

Helen stares at Dr. Harris-Mehta's mouth. The halting way Dr. Harris-Mehta speaks makes it difficult for her to pay attention. She briefly wonders if Mr. Mehta is also a doctor and whether he and Ms. Harris met at medical school. She shakes her head to focus. "Was he alive when he was brought in?"

Dr. Harris-Mehta nods as she twists her wedding band nervously on her finger. "We did everything we could to save your husband. He was never conscious," she repeats, before she says, "We are going to ask you to wait for a few minutes before you see him. Would you like some coffee?" Since she has been on call this morning there has been one emergency after the other. A ten-year-old child chopped his finger off with a hatchet— and what was he doing playing with a hatchet in the first place, she would like to know. A man gashed his leg with a chain saw and to make matters worse he was a diabetic, another kid was having seizures, a little girl got bitten by a dog, and now this. Dr. Harris-Mehta glances toward the reception desk for some help from the nurse, but she is absorbed by her computer screen.

Dr. Harris-Meha's white coat, Helen notices, is buttoned up the wrong way and, briefly, she is tempted to reach over and fix it; she also wonders if this is the first time Dr. Harris-Mehta has had to inform a family member of a death, and a part of her wants to reassure Dr. Harris-Mehta. Alec was no longer her husband; they were no longer close. But this seems too complicated and confusing and also Dr. Harris-Mehta may not yet understand about divorce.

"Was he—had he been drinking?" Helen has to focus again to ask.

"We are running some tests and I am sure the police are investigating."

On the way home in the car, after she was shown Alec in the hospital morgue—afraid of what she might see, Helen had barely looked at the face of the man lying under the white sheet, who now she worries could have been nearly anyone. The dead man had seemed very small and Alec was over six feet tall, but the hair on his head looked the same. Unruly and still mostly red. Helen tries to think about Tuscany again. In San Gimignano, she went to the *duomo* several times to look at Ghirlandaio's frescoes of Santa Fina, the patron saint of the city who, since she was paralyzed from childhood, had to lie immobile for years on a wooden plank. According to legend, when she finally died and her body was removed, the plank was found to be covered with white violets. All of a sudden, Helen remembers the name of the woman who was killed with Alec in the car. Eugenie.

"How was your day?" Harold Mehta asks his wife when she gets home from the hospital. He is not a doctor but an assistant professor of law at the local university; however he and his wife did meet in college. They have been married five years and, next year, when Barbara has finished her residency, they plan to start a family.

"Awful, I'm beat," Barbara answers, shaking her head. "What is today anyway? Is today Friday, the thirteenth?" Barbara tries to smile. "The worst was a car accident. You should have seen him, Harold—the man had severed his aorta. When we opened him up, all the blood that had accumulated in the chest cavity came pouring out, like a wave. A tidal wave. I've never seen anything like it. I had to tell his wife, and I blanked on her name."

"Oh, honey . . . ," Harold starts to say.

"The wife just sat there listening to me while I told her about her husband," Barbara continues, "with no expression on her face, as if I was giving her the weather report or something." Again Barbara tries to smile.

"She was probably in shock," Harold says.

"I guess I should start dinner," Barbara answers.

"Let's go out," Harold tells her. "Someone at school told me about a good Italian restaurant. We could try going there."

The Italian restaurant is where Gina works and she is Harold and Barbara's waitress.

Again, today, she was late for her shift and the restaurant manager gave her a look. Gina knows what the look means: *If you keep this up, sweetheart, you are going to be fired.* But today, Gina does not care: *Let the asshole fire me. See if I give a shit!* She and Craig had a fight and have broken up. And the fight, like most fights, was over something stupid. The fault of seeing that accident, Gina also thinks, which had upset her. As they walked on the beach, Craig started talking again about taking time off to go sailing and Gina told him how she did not want to be stuck on a boat with just one person for a whole year. Of course she did not mean for it to sound quite like that—the "just one person" part—but Craig took offense and he accused her of all sorts of stuff that was not true, or only half true. *Anyway, to hell with him,* Gina thinks as she starts to tell her customers the specials. She barely looks at them as she recommends the fish of the day, which is baked swordfish, the linguine with fresh clams and the veal piccata.

"I'll have the veal," Harold tells Gina.

"And I'll have the linguine," Barbara says.

"Good choices," Gina answers automatically and not smiling. In the mood she is in, she cannot bear to look at couples, especially couples who appear happy together.

"I think I've seen her before," Harold tells Barbara after Gina has left with their order. "On campus. She's a student, maybe."

"Who?"

"The waitress."

"I didn't notice. Is she pretty?" Barbara asks.

"I guess, in a surly sort of way. But not my type," Harold adds. He knows that Barbara is tired and he has to be careful but all of a sudden he remembers why the waitress looks familiar. One morning last fall he was sitting in the school parking lot listening to the end of *Morning Edition* on the radio and to Garrison Keillor list the famous people whose birthdays fell on that day—it was the birthday of Giuseppe Verdi—when he heard someone yell "Bastard!" then a car door slam. Then the waitress—he was ready to bet anything that it was she—ran in front of Harold's car and, as she did so, she must also have stumbled or twisted her ankle because she nearly fell and during the time it took her to recover Harold got a good look at her face. A face, he thought, like in one in those old Italian religious paintings. A moment or two later, a colleague of Harold who was married, only not married to the waitress, and the same person who recommended the restaurant got out of the car.

"Before I went out to speak to the wife," Barbara goes on, as if she were just now finishing her sentence, "I had to change my clothes—not just my coat but my shirt and the pants I was wearing underneath. Everything was soaked with blood."

"Do you want a glass of wine?" Harold asks. He wants to change the subject.

"Even my shoes," Barbara says.

"Red or white?"

Barbara looks up at him. She is frowning.

"Red or white," Harold repeats. He and Barbara rarely drink, only on special occasions like weddings or anniversaries.

Barbara shakes her head. "The man was drunk," she continues. "The police report showed that the blood alcohol content was three times the limit."

"Maybe the accident was intentional."

Again, Barbara shakes her head. "You always assume the worst, don't you?"

"Suicide is not necessarily the worst. If someone no longer has any options. Maybe he was sick with something. Like cancer."

"No. He did not have cancer. Nothing was wrong with him. And what about his wife?"

Harold shrugs as their food arrives. A different waitress, an older waitress, brings them their plates.

"The veal?" She asks smiling and holding the plate up in the air.

"For me," Harold tells her.

"Enjoy your dinner, folks," the waitress says, before she leaves.

"Is she the one?" Barbara asks, although she knows that she is not.

"No. It was someone else," Harold answers, humoring Barbara. Then, as if he had only now come to this decision, he leans across the table and takes Barbara's hand. Squeezing it, he says, "You know something, honey, we're lucky."

Although late in the day when Helen gets home from the hospital, she sets up her easel and paints again on the deck. Determined to distract herself and not to brood on events, she studies the picture she has begun. Helen does not presume to copy Ghirlandaio's painting—she plans to use it as inspiration. For instance, instead of having Santa Fina dressed in red, she is going to paint her naked; instead of having her lie on a wooden plank, she will have her lying in a field of white flowers; she has not yet decided how she will depict Saint Gregory, who has come to Santa Fina as a vision to predict her imminent death. Absorbed as she is, Helen nevertheless is reminded of the life class she took with Alec and how rigorous and old-fashioned Alec's teaching had been. She remembers how adamant he was about proportions—he used the height of the model's head to show them how the rest of the model's body lined up and eight heads was what he said was the norm.

"Measure, measure, measure!" he had shouted at them.

"Does Pablo Picasso measure?" Helen, all stiffness and resentment, asked Alec that first lesson.

"Of course, he measures," Alec replied, looking past Helen at her easel and shaking his head.

In the end, she had surprised herself and learned a lot from Alec. If only, she thinks, she had not married him, but Alec, sober, was hard to resist. Helen sighs as she calculates the length of Santa Fina's body, her elbows at her waist, her arms bent in a position of prayer before she puts her brush to the canvas.

"If only you two had stayed married," on the phone, Daphne kept repeating to Helen, "this would never have happened!" while Helen said nothing. "Despite all his faults," Daphne wailed, "he was a good man. A talented man!" Still Helen had said nothing. In back of her, she can hear the barn swallow chicks in their nest, twittering, anxiously waiting to be fed. Another thing that had attracted Helen to him was that Alec did not have a self-conscious bone in his body. She remembers the time when the model was late and Alec, without saying a word to anyone, took off his clothes and assumed the poses. That day, after class, she also remembers, was when they went back to her house and, for the first time, made love.

And Alec had a nice common touch (later Helen was irritated by it): he always treated everyone exactly the same no matter who they were or how rich they were. Often, he would stop to talk to a waitress or the cashier in a store—invariably, a woman, Helen recalls—for several minutes and when Helen became impatient and accused him of making needless chatter, Alec defended himself by saying that he was just being friendly.

At the trial, she discovered that Eugenie had been employed as a pastry chef at one of the better restaurants on the island and that she was Canadian. Except for a half brother who made threatening faces and gestures at Alec and who, after being warned repeatedly by the judge not to, had to be removed from the courtroom, Eugenie had, it seemed, no other relatives. Even after Helen confronted Alec with receipts—two for a motel on the North Fork and one for a hundred-dollar gift certificate at Neiman Marcus—she found crumpled up in his sports coat pocket, he still continued to deny his affair with Eugenie. The gift certificate, he claimed, was for her, only he misplaced it. Eventually, however, he admitted that on the fatal night, he did have a drink with Eugenie. One drink, he swore to Helen, but, by then, she had stopped believing him.

* * *

When the sun begins to set and the mosquitoes start coming out, Helen can no longer concentrate on her painting and she starts to pack up her paints and fold her easel. As she carries her things around to the front door, she runs into Craig, who is coming home.

"Hi, Mrs. Mallory—can I help carry your stuff?"

Helen had not heard Craig's truck and he has startled her. In the fading evening light, he looks a little like the way Helen imagines Alec might have looked when he was young and Craig's age, although of course she had not known Alec then. Tall, thin, with the same sort of hair.

"Thanks," Helen stammers, "that's nice of you—it's getting dark and too buggy out. Oh—" An unexpected sharp pain in her chest makes her cry out. The pain is like a stab from a knife and Helen has never experienced anything like it. For a moment, she is afraid she is going to fall as, at the same time, unbidden, the image of Alec lying in the hospital morgue comes into her head.

"Are you okay?" Craig asks, putting out his hand to take her arm.

Doubled up outside her house in the near dark, Helen does not answer. She could at least have told him good-bye.

"Are you all right?" Craig repeats. He does not know what to do.

She could have stayed in the room with him and kept him company for a little longer, she thinks, as, slowly, she straightens herself up. Craig's arm, she sees, is outstretched toward her and she is tempted to take it. Instead, she hands him her canvas. "Careful—the paint is still wet," she manages to say.

"Your painting?" Craig holds out Helen's painting without looking at it. After dropping Gina off at work, he had driven around aimlessly all afternoon in his truck. Twice he had gone to Montauk and back. He finds it hard to believe that during the course of a single day his feelings can change so rapidly from love to hate. Like the man in the car, he thinks, one minute you are okay and alive, the next you are dead.

"Of Santa Fina," Helen is saying. The pain has disappeared as quickly as it appeared and she is recovered.

"Santa who?" Craig has understood Helen to say Gina and he looks down at the painting in his hand—a painting of a naked woman lying on a bed of flowers and a man, also naked except for a blue cape thrown over his shoulders, floating over her.

Helen stands holding the front door of her house open for Craig. "She's the patron saint of San Gimignano, where I was in Tuscany," Helen explains. "Have you been to Italy?"

Craig shakes his head. "I wish," he says.

"You can set everything down over there," Helen tells him, taking one more quick, critical look at her painting. "I haven't finished yet and I haven't gotten Saint Gregory quite right."

Craig nods but says nothing.

"Would you like something? A drink?" Helen asks all of a sudden. "I'm going to have something. A gin and tonic."

"A gin and tonic would be fine," Craig says.

Helen goes into the kitchen and Craig can hear her opening cupboards, getting ice, as he stands in the living room and looks around. The only other time he has been in Helen's house, he was so intent on renting the cottage and making a good impression that he barely looked at anything in the room. Now, he notices that all the pictures on the walls are of ships. Most are prints, a few are watercolors and there is one picture that looks like it is made from woven wool.

When Helen returns with the two glasses of gin and tonic, Craig is still looking at the pictures. "Yes, my husband—my"—she starts to identify which husband but changes her mind—"he collected pictures of boats. He loved to sail."

"They're nice," Craig says.

"Sit down, sit down," Helen tells him. She points to an armchair across from where she sits on the sofa. "Make yourself comfortable."

As soon as Craig has sat down across from Helen, Helen's cat jumps up and settles on Craig's lap and, although Craig does not particularly like cats, he strokes the cat's back. Again, Craig is reminded of the accident and of the man having convulsions. When Craig had put the car into reverse, the neighbor had run out of her house just in time to see him back up over the cat. And although Craig had done his best to try to explain that he was putting the cat out of his misery, the neighbor never did believe him.

"I love to sail, too," he begins.

After Craig has left, Helen washes the glasses and dishes —in the end she made Craig and herself some supper— then, after making certain the cat is still inside, she goes around the house locking up. When she gets to the back door she decides to go and take another quick look at the barn swallow nest—with Craig there, she had nearly forgotten about them—before going up to bed. The nest seems strangely quiet and there is no sign of the parents. Could all the chicks have fledged that afternoon while she was painting? Helen wonders. Despite everything she has read that warns against doing this, Helen goes back in the house and gets a step stool and a flashlight—she is just going to have a tiny peek. Taking off her shoes and trying to make as little noise as possible—she sways a little as she climbs up the step stool and has to reach out to the wall of the house for balance, the result of the gin and tonics—she turns on the flashlight when her head is level with the nest. The nest is not empty as she had feared but swarming with tiny bugs—bird mites—and the five barn swallow chicks inside it are dead.

From his bed in the cottage, Craig cannot sleep. He drank too many gin and tonics and he feels a little sick to his stomach. Also, he talked too much and he feels embarrassed. And each time he shuts his eyes, he again sees the wrecked car and the man convulsing on the stretcher. And it is exceedingly hot in his room. Getting out of bed, Craig opens the window wider to try to let in more air. As he does this, he hears a strange sound coming from across the lawn, from Helen's house. A woman crying.

My Flame

.

The ringing phone woke them.

"Who the hell is that?" Mark asked, sitting up in bed.

"I don't know. Hello? Hello," Alison repeated.

"Who? Oh, Leslie."

"Leslie?" Mark said. "What time is it?"

"Sssh, wait." She motioned to him with her hand, although, in the dark, he could not see it. "What's wrong?" she said.

"Tell Leslie it's the middle of the fucking night," Mark said, lying back down hard and making the mattress bounce. Outside, the headlights of a car briefly illumined one wall of the room and the dresser on which there stood a photograph of two small boys and a glass jar filled with change.

After she had hung up the phone, she turned on the light.

"My sister Janine is a drunk, a poor sad drunk," his eyes squeezed shut, Mark said. "They should lock her up. Can you turn out the damn light."

"Poor Leslie," she said.

"How old is she?"

"I don't know. Fourteen, fifteen. We saw her last Christmas."

"Shit," Mark also said, reaching over to push up Alison's nightgown, "now, I will never go back to sleep."

Years later, in another country, France, in another city, Paris, she will have completely forgotten about that night. Long since divorced, she rarely thinks about Mark or Leslie, who, in any case, are both dead. The only thing left to her from that time is the photograph of the two small boys—grown men now—which stands in a silver frame on top of the mantelpiece in her apartment, located a stone's throw from the Luxembourg Garden, on rue Madame.

Seconds after he rolled off her, he fell asleep.

In one dream, he is riding a motorcycle on a mountainous road. The hairpin turns, the low twisted guardrails on the cliff side of the road, the view of the sea below, remind him of the corniche above the coast of the Riviera and of a summer years ago when he had sailed in the Mediterranean. But then the scenery in the dream abruptly changes, and he is riding his motorcycle through a village—a village that could be in England, in say the Cotswolds, where he has never been but of which he has seen pictures—with thatched-roofed cottages all lined up in a row, their tidy gardens filled with roses and tall hollyhocks. As he rides by, someone in one of the cottages calls out his name. He thinks it is his mother. Then the door of the cottage opens, and a little girl of about four or five with long blonde hair runs out into the street before he has time to stop. The woman who had called to him, who is not his mother and whom he does not recognize, shouts to him that it is his fault the little girl has been killed.

When, later, he awoke and for a few moments recollected his dream, he also remembered a day during that long-ago Mediterranean summer when he and a girl, who were both the crew on a Concordia yawl—he cannot recall her name, only what she looked like: small, with strong calf muscles (he can still see her balancing on the deck, even in rough weather, to adjust a jib sheet), and her curly hair—had taken a taxi to a village above Cannes and had lunch at an inn someone had recommended. At the inn, L'Auberge du Midi, or a name like that, the girl and Mark had helped themselves to *pâté de campagne* from a big earthenware crock, next to a large platter of little pink *écrevisses* they dipped into bright yellow mayonnaise, then a lamb cassoulet, cheeses, a homemade peach tart for dessert; and they had drunk wine, a rosé from the region served in a carafe, and it was the best meal he had ever eaten in his life. He would never forget that. Funny what one remembered and the curly-haired girl whose name he has forgotten and who he had wanted to sleep with but never did.

On a Greyhound bus, on her way to Mark and Alison's house, which was a few miles outside the District, in Virginia, Leslie could not sleep. Her little Yorkshire terrier, Suzy, was stuffed under her seat in a tote bag. From time to time, the dog whined and although the bus was not crowded, Leslie worried someone might complain. Finally, taking advantage of the darkness, she took Suzy out of the bag and put her on her lap, half-covering her with her jacket.

"Sssh, sssh." She patted the dog's head.

On the phone, she had not told Alison about Suzy. About bringing her. Now, she hoped Alison would not mind. Alison was very kind but you never knew about people and how they felt about dogs, although her dog,

Suzy, was no trouble. She was a sweet dog and Leslie could never give her up. Especially now. When Leslie thought about her mother and how, drunk, her mother had on various occasions threatened her with violence, she started to cry again.

Although it is cold and windy, Alison was standing outside of the bus station. The waiting room had been crowded with homeless people trying to keep warm; one man was stretched out full length on a bench, the fly open on his stained pants. She hoped the bus would not be late as it was her day to carpool, and in less than an hour she had to pick up the twins at school. Then she had to drive them to hockey practice. Meantime, she had made up the bed in the guest room for Leslie. She had made it up with her best sheets—fancy European sheets with a pretty flower pattern and scalloped borders—to make Leslie feel welcome. Also, she had put pink towels in the bathroom and a new bar of perfumed soap. In addition, she spent most of the day on the phone, getting transcripts from Leslie's old school and making the arrangements at the local one. Mark, too, had had to make several calls. Shivering, Alison pulled her coat more tightly around her as she scanned the street for the bus. Who knew? It might be nice, for a change, to

have another female in the house. Although shy, Leslie
seemed like a sweet girl. Life with alcoholic Janine was
certainly no picnic and her husband, Leslie's stepfather,
Anders—he was Swedish—was gone most of the year,
mapping poverty in Senegal or Mali or somewhere in
Africa, when Alison thought he should have been home
mapping the wrongs in his own house. At dinner, the last
time she saw Anders, he had been rude and dismissive.
What had he said to her: that she was overly deferential?
Unjustified, yet the remark had rankled. Perhaps, he, too,
had been drunk. Janine, she remembered, had quarreled
loudly with Mark during the meal, then had passed out
on the sofa. At last, the bus came into view and Alison
got ready to wave.

The twins were more interested in Suzy than in Leslie.
Before supper, laughing wildly at each other, they took
turns throwing a tennis ball for the little dog outside in
the garden, making her fetch it. The ball was thrown
harder and farther and, each time, the dog was made
more agitated, jumping up on her hind legs and barking incessantly, until Alison went outside and called the
game to a halt. "Enough," she said, "it's cold and the
dog is getting overexcited." Throughout their game, Leslie had stood at the living room window, watching, not

daring to interfere. The boys' exuberance intimidated her. She also did not want to alienate them. The twins were eight at the time and years later, when their mother told them how their cousin Leslie had been killed in a car accident while her dog—no doubt, by then, a different dog—who was also in the car survived unhurt, would have almost no memory of either Leslie or her little dog. "You don't remember how she stayed in the guest room for months and her dog barked all the time and made me crazy?" Alison persisted. The thing that Peter, one of the twins, said he remembered best about that time was getting knocked out in the hockey rink—although he cannot actually remember that either—only the aftermath: the doctor asking him stupid questions like how many fingers was he holding up in front of his face and asking him to count backwards from twenty-five, as apparently he had suffered a mild concussion. While Sam, more conscientious, and always slightly prescient, had asked Alison: "Was she drinking?"

Sam does remember Leslie. In fact he will never forget how one night, afraid it would rain, he got out of bed and went to get his bicycle, which he had left lying outside in the garden, and as he walked past the guest bathroom window—both the guest bedroom and bathroom were

situated downstairs in the house and the windows gave
out onto the garden in back, which was private so there
was no real need to draw the blinds—he saw that the
bathroom light was on. Standing on his tiptoes, Sam
peered inside. Leslie was running herself a bath, and
he watched as she took off her clothes, her panties and
her bra, exposing her already large breasts, her fat belly
and her hairy mound, which was much darker than the
blonde hair on her head. He watched her get into the
tub, and then he watched as she positioned herself in
the water in such a way that her legs were spread and
up in the air and the water from the taps was running
in between them. Leslie's head was resting on the side
of the tub, her eyes were shut and, all of a sudden, she
cried out. Frightened, Sam must have cried out, too,
as he ran inside the house, for he could hear Leslie
call out, "Who's there?" He wanted to tell Peter, but
Peter was already asleep when he got back to their
room, and also, the next day, he was not sure how to
describe what he had seen. From then on, however,
every time he saw Leslie, eating her Special K in the
morning or after she had come home from school
and was watching TV or as they were all eating dinner together, he could never quite rid himself of the
image of her naked in the tub, her legs spread up in
the air. As a result, he avoided her.

*   *   *

Opening the front door to his house that first evening, Mark heard a dog barking. "What the hell is that?" he said out loud to himself. "Pete, Sam! Boys!" He called out to the twins before he saw Leslie standing in the hall. She held the dog in her arms.

"Oh, Leslie?" Preoccupied at work, Mark had forgotten about Leslie. A French cheese maker was a prospective client but as yet he had not closed on the deal. La Vache Qui Rit, he kept repeating the name to himself in his head.

"Welcome," he said, recovering himself. He wanted to be friendly to the girl. "Is that your dog?" he asked.

"Suzy." Half-offering up the dog in her arms to Mark, Leslie also said, "Thank you, Uncle Mark, for having me come stay with you. I can't tell you how much I . . ." Leslie was afraid she would start to cry again.

"No, no, don't worry about it. It's not a problem." Mark leaned down and patted Leslie on the shoulder. "We're glad to have you." Since he had last seen her, Leslie, Mark noticed, had gained a lot of weight. "Does your dog bite?" He wanted to make light of the moment.

"Oh, no, Suzy is very sweet."

"That's good to know." Mark smiled at Leslie. "Where's Alison? Where are the boys? In the kitchen?"

*   *   *

Left alone in the house—Mark had left for work, Alison, too, was gone, as twice a week she volunteered at the Hirshhorn Museum, the twins were in school and Leslie had begun junior high that morning—Suzy chewed the fringe off the living room carpet, an antique, orange, blue and yellow patterned kilim Mark and Alison had bought on their honeymoon, in Turkey, from a rug dealer named Mohammed. She then threw it back up, half digested, on the carpet. She also shat—she had diarrhea by then—in the hallway, the dining room, the kitchen and in Leslie's bedroom. Days later, the dog, Suzy, would have no memory of this—only perhaps a slight instinctive reaction of shame, so that each time she saw Alison, she slunk past her.

Mark claimed that he fell in love with Alison's voice. The minute he heard it on the phone, when she had called to tell him that she had found his wallet lying on the stairs—she had specified the stairs in between the second and third floors—of her college dormitory. Right away, Mark said, the sound of her voice gave him a hard-on. "Gross," was how later Alison had replied when he told her, although a part of her had been flattered and wanted to believe him. The wallet had contained a driver's license, nineteen dollars in five- and one-dollar bills, a laundry receipt, a receipt for $13.34 from the college co-op, and two packages of condoms, also a photo of a girl in a striped bathing suit. The same girl Mark later told Alison he had gone up, taking the stairs two at a time in his hurry, to visit in the dormitory when the wallet must have dropped out of his pocket. "My flame," was how he referred to the girl and never by her name.

Ma flamme, Alison repeats softly to herself on her way to the *boulangerie* on rue de Fleurus, a few doors down from where Gertrude Stein and Alice B. Toklas used to live. Something must have triggered the memory: perhaps the bit of brown paper lying on the sidewalk that for a moment she mistook for a wallet. When they started going out together, Mark had called her that as well: it was how he introduced her to his friends—"My flame." How many flames had he had in his life? she wonders. A forest fire's worth, she thinks, and she pictures huge orange flames licking up and consuming great tall trees that then, in her mind, turn into a blackened destroyed area, an area of total desolation, as she opens the door to the *boulangerie* and breathes in the odor of freshly baked bread.

*   *   *

The fancy imported sheets with the pretty flower pattern and scalloped borders were of little comfort to Leslie. The second night, she got her period in the middle of the night—early and, no doubt, due to stress—and stained them. In a panic, she stripped the bed and ran the sheets under cold water in the tub, scrubbing them as hard as she could with the scented soap, then she hung them over the pink towels to dry. Still, she could make out the darker outlines of the stains.

In the department store dressing room, Leslie sat fully dressed on the little bench staring at herself in the mirror, only occasionally getting up to make rustling noises in order to appear to be trying on the clothes. "Nothing really fits," she called out after a while.

"Are you sure? Do you want to show me?" From outside the dressing room door, Alison called back. "Or shall I get you another size? A bigger size?"

"No. No, thank you, Aunt Alison," Leslie answered, examining her face more closely in the mirror. "They're just not my style."

"Well, why don't you have another look," Alison

persisted. "I saw some really cute capri pants and some neat shirts. I am sure you will like them."

"It's okay, Aunt Alison. I'm fine." Leslie squeezed a pimple on her forehead, spattering pus on the mirror.

"You're sure?"

"Yes, Aunt Alison."

It wasn't that Leslie did not like Alison. On the contrary, she did. She liked her a lot and she admired her. Her calm, her good humor, her perfect figure. She admired how organized everything in her house was and how clean; the healthy fresh food, the meals always on time. The way, too, Alison handled the boys and their rowdiness. She never seemed to get angry, only, at times, irritated. There was never any shouting. Also, Leslie admired how well Alison and Mark seemed to get along. She did not appear to mind that he did most of the talking, and when he told jokes he made her laugh in a particular way, as if perhaps she was laughing in spite of herself or against her better judgment. On most weekends, they played tennis together. In the evenings, when Mark came home, they always kissed on the lips, even if Mark was late. In the car, on the way home, Alison was telling Leslie about her day at the museum and how she had taken a group of tourists through the Henry Moore sculpture exhibit.

"Do you know his work?" Alison asked.

Leslie had not been listening. "What?"

"The sculptor, Henry Moore. The tourists were Japanese," Alison went on, "and at the end of the tour, I asked the tour leader if anyone had any questions about what they had seen, and after he had translated what I had said, a lady in the group raised her hand"—Alison looked over at Leslie—"and you know what she asked?"

"No, what?" Again, Leslie was only half-listening.

"She asked if now that they were finished with the tour, could they go to a shopping mall. Can you believe that?" Alison was shaking her head and laughing.

In bed, Alison put down her book and said, "I'm worried about her. After school, I tried to take her shopping but she wouldn't let me buy her clothes. She should lose weight, but of course I didn't say anything."

"Who are you talking about?" Mark asked. "Leslie?"

"Yes. It's too bad, the twins kind of ignore her. The dog, too, is making me a little crazy."

Mark laughed. "Shoot it, " he said.

"But I'm serious about Leslie. I want her to be happy here."

"Don't worry about her. She'll adjust. It takes time sometimes." Mark said. "Turn out the light, will you? I have to get up really early tomorrow and meet a client."

"Who?"

"La Vache Qui Rit."

"Who?"

"A French cheese company. It means 'the cow that laughs.'"

"I know." Alison said. "I know that much French." In her head, she could not help picturing a slender Frenchwoman. The Frenchwoman was smiling at Mark.

Every day, Leslie wore the same thing: stretch pants and an oversized man's shirt. The only clothes she could fit into and feel comfortable in. Luckily the school did not have a dress code. All the kids wore jeans. So far, Leslie had not met anyone except in a casual way—a few girls she could ask about an assignment, or whether a teacher was strict or the location of a classroom but not much more. Many of the kids in her class, and the teachers, too, spoke with a thick southern accent and she had trouble understanding them. And a lot of the girls in her class who were her age, fourteen, she noticed, wore eye makeup and were going out with boys—they wore their rings, their sweatshirts, they clung to each other in the halls and kissed. Outside the school they smoked cigarettes, some of them smoked pot. Leslie heard the girls talk about the boys—how they made out together, some of them boasted about going all the way. If the parents were not there, they had all-night parties. They drank.

Leslie, too, began to drink in spite of what she already knew firsthand about the effects of alcohol and, no doubt, due to what a costly shrink would later point out were her "self-destructive" tendencies, while she was staying at Mark and Alison's house. Nights, when she was sure everyone was in bed, she would sneak into the dining room and open the liquor cabinet. Barefoot, in her pajamas, she stood in the dark and drank straight out of the bottle: whiskey, rum, gin, vodka, liqueurs—she did not care what it was. The alcohol burned her throat and helped her go to sleep. One night, she did not hear Mark come quietly down the stairs. Before she could move, he turned on the light. He was pointing a .22 rifle at her.

"Christ, Leslie!" he yelled. "I thought you were a burglar. What the hell are you doing in here?"

Alison looked forward to the two days, Tuesday and Thursday, she volunteered at the Hirshhorn. Not only did they get her out of the house, but they brought her close to art. Before she married Mark, she had wanted to be an artist, and she still hoped that one day, after the twins were grown, she could go back to painting. Her teachers had encouraged her and told her she had talent.

For a while, when she and Mark were first married, she had hung some of the paintings she had made as a student in the house—abstract paintings of blue and green stripes that were heavily influenced by Richard Diebenkorn, her favorite painter—but after a while Alison had taken them down. She thought the paintings were bad and they made her sad.

In Paris, Alison shares a studio with a woman called Bernadette. Bernadette sits at a table in a corner of the room and does mostly decorative découpages, cutting pictures out of old books and magazines that she artfully glues together, frames and sells. Bernadette also has a house in the south of France, and often she is away from Paris for months at a time. The studio is in the Nineteenth Arrondissement, in a nondescript old building. To get to it, Alison has to cross a courtyard full of cast-off appliances and car parts and then, even in the rain, she has to climb a rickety wooden outdoor staircase. Once inside, she forgets the world, her life, Bernadette, and she paints. One whole wall of the studio is made of glass.

Leslie's room was a mess. Her clothes were strewn on the floor, along with her school books and papers. A wet towel was draped over an upholstered chair. The bed was unmade—the blanket and the bedspread were bunched up on top of the mattress. The dog was lying on Leslie's jacket, which lay on the floor; also spread on the floor were sheets of newspapers. Inside the bathroom, Mark could hear the drip of a faucet.

"Don't tell Aunt Alison." Leslie had started to cry.

Sitting down on the unmade bed, Mark patted the spot next to him. "Tell me what is going on? Do you want to go home?"

Shaking her head, Leslie said, "No. I just feel—I don't know, Uncle Mark, I can't explain."

"Try," Mark said.

"Thank god, I did not see him get knocked out," Alison would later tell Mark. "Apparently, he just lay there on his back on the ice in a pool of blood."

"Head wounds bleed a lot," Mark said.

Instead, the doctor had called her from the hospital, which was probably no less worrisome, although he, Dr. Delmonico, had tried to reassure her. Peter, he was 99 percent sure, he said, would be fine. Nonetheless that 1 percent caused Alison to drive a hundred miles an hour from her house to the hospital.

"Lucky, I didn't get a ticket," she also told Mark.

"Or have an accident," he said. "You might have ended up next to Pete."

To make certain, Dr. Delmonico wanted to keep Peter in the hospital overnight, and Alison had stayed with him, in his room. Meantime, she arranged for Sam to be picked up from school by a friend, who also volunteered to keep Sam for the night. She had also telephoned Mark, assuring him that Peter would be fine and that his presence was not necessary at the hospital. Relieved, as he still had a lot of work to do, he promised to be home early and to bring home a pizza for Leslie and himself.

Why did he sleep with her? If ever Mark asked himself that question, he was unable to answer it. He wasn't attracted to her. She was not his type, she was overweight. Also, she was much too young. And a virgin. What the hell had he been thinking? And not just once but at least a dozen times. On the weekend when he was home, each time Alison left the house to pick up the twins or go do an errand, he would sneak down to Leslie's room. He would fuck her on her unmade bed, the damn dog whining somewhere underneath the bed. Partly he felt sorry for her, partly she was willing, or something like that. She wasn't even good in bed; she was too compliant, too passive. Probably she was frightened. He, too, may have been attracted by the danger of it. Part of him would like to think that it had been a good experience for her, it had given her confidence. It had made her feel womanly and desired or some bullshit like that. Mostly, however, he does not like to think about it.

As soon as he had shut the door to her room and left, Leslie whispered to herself, "Uncle Mark, Uncle Mark." But when they were in bed together, she did not call him Uncle Mark. Nor did she call him Mark. She did not call him anything. He was always in a hurry, not saying much to her except to tell her not to worry, that he was the one who took precautions, and that he would not hurt her, although sometimes he did. He never got completely undressed either, he kept his shirt on while they had sex, and most of the time Leslie kept her eyes shut. The worst was afterward, when she saw him in the house, with Alison and the twins, at dinnertime or during the breakfast rush, behaving as if nothing had happened, as if he had not touched her breasts or put his penis in her mouth, asking her to pass the salt or asking how she had done on an algebra test. All the time she hardly dared look at him, and her heart was pounding so hard and fast she was afraid she would faint or drop dead. Of course, too, she always felt horribly guilty toward Alison, betraying her like that in her own house and taking advantage of her kindness. In addition, she worried that Alison would find out. But, perhaps as, later on, Leslie began to suspect, Alison knew. In the years to come, Leslie always told herself, and told her costly shrink whom she saw twice a week—and this may have been only an excuse—that she was in love with Mark. Uncle Mark. He was so good-looking, so energetic, so kind and understanding. She could not help it, she said. And he, too, must have loved her.

If, from time to time—times that are now marked by longer and longer intervals, especially since she lives in Paris and her life is so removed from what it once was— Alison thinks about Mark, she does not think about him with bitterness or with any ire, especially now that he has died. Instead she tends to think about him quite fondly. Like an old family friend or perhaps like a beloved old dog. She has concluded that Mark was a romantic, that he was an egotist, and that he never thought to do harm. He simply did not think. Also, she has forgotten what it was like to be married to him, and the twelve years are reduced to what amounts to probably only a few minutes of memories, so that sometimes she feels almost cheated. She could never, like the French prisoner Papillon, confined to years of solitary confinement, recall the events of her life minute by minute. No never. Instead she remembers random unimportant things like Mark singing. He had a nice voice and he took such pleasure belting out the verses of his favorite hymn: "Bring me my bow of burning gold! / Bring me my arrows of desire!" Ah, desire, Alison thinks, smiling. She is painting in her studio in the Nineteenth Arrondissement. Recently, her canvases have become more and more abstract. The one she is presently working on depicts a large round brown mass with a bright electric-yellow background.

Coming over to look at it, Bernadette puts her hand on Alison's shoulder and remarks that it is *très violent*. What will Alison call the painting? Bernadette also wants to know.

Without thinking about it, Alison replies, "Accident."

Alison also remembers the time Mark proposed to her. It was an August night and they were lying on the beach together looking up at the stars. Alison was determined to see a shooting star so that she could make a wish—perhaps a wish that Mark would ask her to marry him. Then they made love on the stony beach. Now, of course, she cannot recall if she had actually seen a shooting star that night and made her wish. Nor, worse still, can Alison recall Mark's lovemaking.

The accident occurred when Leslie was thirty-one. Leslie was on her way home after she had been drinking several whiskey sours at a bar in town called the Buena Vista, and the road was icy because, earlier that evening, it had snowed. Leslie was driving too fast, and her car skidded out of control around a corner and hit a tree. She was killed instantly. Alison only learned about Leslie's death several months later while she was buying a newspaper at a kiosk in the Gare de Lyon.

"Alison! Hello!" A man called out to her. "It's Anders. Remember? Janine's husband. Ex-husband." He laughed. Anders's hair had gone gray and he had grown a beard, which was also gray. Alison would never have recognized him.

"I always felt sorry for her," Alison told Anders.

Anders shook his head. "She seemed to be having a pretty good time screwing Mark in your—" Anders stopped himself. "Hey. I thought you knew. I thought that was why you and Mark got divorced."

In her seat in the first-class section of the train, on her way to visit Bernadette, whose house is located in a small hilltop village called Pierrefeu, near Toulon, Alison was surprised, after all these years, at how shocked and duped she felt.

Outside, it was drizzling. "Bastard," she repeated. The train picked up speed, and suddenly before she had a chance to realize it, they were already in the country. They passed a thick forest of trees, then an open field dotted with red poppies, then more fields filled with sunflowers.

She and Leslie had gone shopping together again, and that last time Leslie had let Alison buy her clothes. A black polka-dot party dress with a full skirt and a bit of a plunging neckline. By then it was late spring and the end of the school year and Leslie had lost weight; her complexion had cleared up. At home, when she showed off the new dress, Mark had twirled her around the living room, making the polka-dot skirt flare out. He promised her that all the boys were going to fall in love her.

The sun was trying to come out, and the sunflowers appeared a bright, almost unnatural neon yellow, their heads all nodding in the same direction. In the distance, Alison saw a village, a church, a large turreted house surrounded by a stone wall, then more fields filled with sunflowers, then fields with cattle and horses. Everything looked green and fresh and well cared for. Not slowing down, the train went hurtling by a row of white houses. Behind the lowered barrier, Alison could see the stopped cars, a man on a tractor, some children waving at the train. From where she sat, Alison waved back, but she was too late.

Bloomsday in Bangkok

In June, after Frank had left, Claire saw monkeys, monkeys instead of people. She saw them sitting behind the
wheels of cars, she saw them swinging golf clubs, she
saw them doing the twist—*Lock to the light, lock to the reft,*
she mimicked how the Thais sang, how they transported
the *l*s for the *r*s and vice versa.

   She, James and Frank had once spent an afternoon
mimicking how, on a visit to Bangkok's floating market, Vice President Lyndon B. Johnson, with both hands
touching his forehead and joined as if in prayer, ignoring
protocol and uninvited, was said to have jumped into a
vendor's tippy little boat. First, it was Claire's turn, and
with the serious look she might put on for a funeral,
she made an exaggeratedly awkward leap next to where
James was sitting in the living room. The result of this
leap was to send James, as the vendor, into a violent

paroxysm of rocking, while Frank, as the bystander, contorted his face to show horror. Then they switched roles. Frank was Claire and James's best friend. Frank was a captain in the U.S. Army; he went away for long periods of time up-country not telling them where—to Laos, probably.

Claire and James made a point of living differently from the other Americans and living the way the Thais—they referred to them as Siamese—did. They took off their shoes before going inside their house, they eschewed air-conditioning in favor of ceiling fans, they went without hot water—to wash her hair which then was long, Claire went to the Royal Bangkok Sports Club. Once a week, James drove to a Chinese barber on New Road who cut his hair, shaved him and cleaned his ears—the barber inserted a thin blade deep into James's ear, then twirled the blade. Afterward James claimed that he could hear a lot better.

They took small, single-engine planes with names like Otter and Beaver, rode on packed local buses, hitch-hiked in rickety wooden trucks to places like Chiang Mai, Chiang Rai, Pimai. They slept on bamboo mats on the floor of raised thatched houses, they ate the eyes of fish, the testicles of roosters, thousand-year-old duck eggs soaked in horses' urine—delicacies reserved for guests—they drank Mekhong, the raw local liquor made from distilled rice (the deposit on the bottle cost more than the liquor itself), they went to the bathroom in thickets, in paddies. They got heatstroke and sunburnt, they got soaked to the skin in sudden downpours, stung by mosquitoes and sucked on by leeches, sick the one time they smoked opium and, of course, they always had diarrhea.

Also, everywhere they went, people stared at them. In the more remote villages, the children—except for one little girl of about eight or nine who ran up and yanked two-handed at Claire's hair as if the long blonde braid were a rope for her to swing on—were frightened and hid from them.

And *Pinai? Pinai?*—Where are you going? the villagers always called out after them.

In her letters home, Claire wrote about the orchids, the jasmine for sale in the market, the purple bougainvillea and the sweet-smelling frangipani growing in their yard. She described the mangoes, mangosteens, papayas, lychee nuts, the twenty-some variety of bananas—she vowed, she wrote, to try each one. Meantime, her friends, Claire imagined, were pushing carts in the supermarket, making piecrusts, changing diapers, while their husbands left their cramped houses, half awake in the mornings, to go to banks, to practice law, to sort mail—one of Claire's friends was married to a postal clerk.

Claire played golf, she swam laps in Frank's pool, she played mah-jongg. The Siamese women she played with, she told Frank and James—*clack, clack*, Claire imitated the sound of the ivory tiles—were so polite that they let her win, and Frank said, "Politeness can kill you," going on to describe how when once he had taken the wrong road to Ubon and had stopped at a village to ask for directions, he was told that *chai, chai*—yes, yes—he was on the right road so that he would not lose face by turning around and going back. "Forty miles out of my way and none of it paved. Can you imagine?" Frank said.

Instead of answering, Claire began to imitate the greedy singsong sound of women counting: *Yii-sip-et, yii-sip-sawng, yii-sip-sam, yii-sip-sii, yii-sip-ha.*

Tow rai?—How much? Claire knew the cost of the *sam-law* ride from her house to the Royal Bangkok Sports Club, where she went to wash her hair—no more than fifteen *baht*. She was also used to how the driver sat catty-corner in his seat and drove out of their lane onto the larger avenue without looking.

Bow bow—Slow down—she shouted to him from the backseat.

Cha cha—which meant the same thing but made no difference.

James drove a Land Rover. He charged the Bangkok traffic, the cars, the *samlaws*, the bicycles—and all but one got out of his way. Lucky for James. The man he hit was an Indian, an Indian delivering *ghee* from a bucket dangling from his handlebars—the ghee had splashed all over the Land Rover's windshield. No matter that it was not James's fault—the Indian had turned without signaling—had he been a Thai, James would have gone straight to prison. Or he would have had to bribe someone.

Siri would have known. Siri was James's Thai partner. Siri knew whom to give a thousand *baht* and a bottle of Johnnie Walker Red to so James and Claire could exchange their tourist visas for resident ones, he knew whom to give another thousand *baht* and another bottle of whiskey to so that they could get their Thai driver's licenses without having to take the test. Siri knew all the officials and he could help James get around the red tape and do business in Thailand. And Thailand, James liked to maintain, had never been a Communist country or colonized and was still unspoiled. He could make a lot of money in Thailand and, at the same time, travel, explore, have a good time.

Sitting around his pool after swimming her laps, Claire complained to Frank about Siri and how she did not trust him.

"Siri is using James. Using James for his money," she said.

But Frank had his own problems. A medic in Vientiane had told him to breathe inside a brown paper bag.

"Yeah, well . . ." Shrugging, Frank pointed to the two planes flying overhead.

"You know what that reminds me of?" he asked. "The time I was twelve and me and my brother were walking home from school. We were still living in South Carolina then, and I happened to look up at the sky. Two jets were flying toward each other—one plane going east to west, the other south to north—and I said to my brother: 'Hey, Tim, look at those jets up there. Wouldn't it be funny if they collided?' And you know what? They did."

"God. What about the passengers?"

"They were Air Force jets. The pilots managed to eject and parachute down, although I don't remember exactly. But the real funny thing is when I mention the two planes colliding to Tim, he swears that he never saw such a thing happen and that I made it up. Or dreamt it. And maybe I did."

"Let's go and play golf," Claire said.

*   *   *

The night before Frank was to go home on leave, they had dinner at an outdoor Chinese restaurant off Sukhumvit Road. James ordered beers, Claire lit a cigarette—she still smoked then—and Frank carefully placed his brown paper bag on the table in front of him.

"You just need to go home and rest for a while," James said.

Not looking at James, Frank said, "Yeah, and guess what? I get to see my dog—my folks' dog now more likely. A border collie. Belle. You should see her, she's a real beauty. She likes to herd people, she's always circling, she can drive you a little nuts, too."

Halfway through the meal, a ripe coconut fell out of a tree next to their table, knocking over bottles and glasses, breaking their dish of sweet and sour prawns, and sending Frank, arms raised to protect his head, out of his chair and under the table.

Once seated again, Frank said, "Sorry about that," and reached for his paper bag.

"Scared the hell out of me, too," James said.

"Take a look at my dress," Claire said, rubbing at the sweet and sour sauce stains.

A week later, Claire received a postcard from Frank. The picture on the postcard was of two white poodle puppies against a bright blue background. Frank had written *Meow meow meow* all over the message part. James, when he read it, said the postcard was a sure sign that Frank was feeling better, and Claire said she missed Frank and she was going to write him a long letter in Thai from Queen Sirikit.

In the Land Rover, on their way to visit Siri and his wife, Sunny, at their weekend bungalow in Pattaya, Claire was doing her imitation of birdcalls. Her favorites, she told James, were the striated woodpecker's and the immature bufflehead's. The road was full of potholes and the day was hot and humid. All of a sudden it began to rain. The rain came down hard and fast and the windshield wipers on the Land Rover were stuck—stuck with *ghee*, Claire guessed—and James had to work them by hand through the open window.

Claire persisted: *Pawk, pawk, pawk.*

"Can you be serious," James said.

"Can you be quiet," James also said.

Claire loved to swim but, in Pattaya, she worried about sharks. The Gulf of Siam, she had heard say, was a breeding ground for them, and she did not dare swim her usual crawl, nor did she dare swim out far. She kept her head out of the water and kept an eye out for a shark fin. Claire also kept looking back at James, who was closer to shore. Once a camp counselor, James was teaching

Siri's wife, Sunny, how to swim. Sunny was slim and pretty. She was wearing a white bathing suit. James had his arms around her and each time a small wave came, Sunny tried to stand up—she did not want to get her hair wet. She was laughing. James, too, was laughing and although Claire could never swear to this—perhaps she imagined it—it looked to her as if each time Sunny raised her head out of the water, James bent his to give Sunny a kiss.

Siri hardly left the bungalow. He liked to cook, he said. Dressed in a chef's tall hat and a long white apron, Siri stayed in the kitchen, cleaning, cutting, chopping food. He was, he told James and Claire, making them the same special Thai dish his mother made for him—a red snapper steamed in coconut husks. Later, at dinner, to show Siri how much he was enjoying the meal, James sucked noisily on the fish bones. He also went on to tell Siri how, in Thailand, he prided himself on his ability to eat everything. Siri then said how he bet he could offer James at least one dish that James would refuse to eat.

"You're on, Siri." James reached across the table with his hand and said, "How much?"

During the meal, Claire asked, "How did you like learning how to swim, Sunny?"

Smiling, Sunny answered that for her cooking and swimming were very much alike and she probably would never learn how to do either one. Then she told Claire how although she had never traveled outside of Thailand, sixty years ago, her grandfather had gone to study in the United States. It took him three months to cross the Pacific Ocean by ship and he stayed away for three years. During that time, his family never once heard from him and they assumed he had drowned.

A month went by and Frank had not returned to Thailand nor had Claire and James heard from him again.

"I am going to telephone someone," Claire said.

"Telephone who?" James said.

"I don't know. A five-star general," Claire answered.

Claire took a *samlaw* to Frank's house. She had to ring the bell several times before the houseboy opened the gate. Dressed in a dirty sarong and still buttoning his shirt, the houseboy barely looked at Claire.

Mai mi, mai mi—Not here—he said.

Glancing past him, Claire could see Frank's swimming pool. The water was a dark green, nearly black, with stuff floating in it. A woman with long untidy hair stood in the doorway of Frank's house staring out at Claire. Claire heard a baby crying.

"What did you expect?" James said after Claire told him what she had seen, "Probably the houseboy's entire family and the houseboy's entire village have moved in while Frank's away. As for the pool, they can clean it up in no time when Frank comes back."

At a cocktail party celebrating the promotion of one of Frank's fellow officers, James and Claire were told how, two weeks after he got home, Frank was taken to the nearest veterans' hospital in Ohio, where his folks lived. Frank, the officer said, had to have electroshock treatment. For morale's sake, the officer had been advised not to mention this, although he felt sure that Frank would be getting an honorable discharge. He would get James and Claire the address of the V.A. hospital, he said. By then Claire had written Frank several letters. In one, she had included her golf scorecard but Frank had not answered.

The golf course was where Claire first noticed the monkeys—how the foursome ahead of her on the fifth hole, the water hole, appeared to be walking on their hands. Claire had to look again. Perhaps one of the men playing had leaned down to pick up a golf ball or had leaned down to retie his shoelace, only it happened a second time. Also Claire noticed something waving in the air that could only be a tail. The tail was not a golf club—not even a slender nine iron. Later, when she went into the women's locker room to wash her hair, the same sort of thing happened there. Noi, the attendant who always handed Claire a clean towel, had for perhaps only a fraction of a second chattered her teeth at her.

At home, she said to James, "Remember how tomorrow we were planning to go and sit around Frank's pool and drink gin and orange juice and read *Ulysses*? Remember, too, how Frank said it was his turn to read all of Molly Bloom?"

"Come on, Claire, you are talking as if Frank is dead," James said.

It was true. Frank had died by then only James and Claire would not hear about his death until later or hear how he had hung himself in his parents' garage with Belle, his border collie's choke chain.

June 16 was also the day Siri had planned on making good on his bet. Siri gave James the address and the directions—the place was not a restaurant. It was someone's house across the river in Thonburi. At first, Claire said she would not go, she would stay home. She was afraid, she said, that she and James would disappear the way Frank had, only it would be different.

But, in the end, she did go, and James lost his bet. Siri broke even. The cost of the monkey, the special table with the hole in the middle, finding a place for the meal, bribing people, James said had come to at least a thousand *baht*—after all, the whole thing was highly illegal. Thank god was what Claire had said. Leaving the house, she had gone to sit by herself in the Land Rover. She had rolled up the car windows and put her fingers to her ears. Still she thought she could hear the whine of the electric saw.

St. Guilhem-le-Désert

The time Anne leaves her husband, she goes to France. She spends the first few days in Paris at an inexpensive hotel on rue Jacob. Her room is small and sparsely furnished; the bathroom, too, is small, the shower produces a tepid trickle. Instead of looking out onto the street, the single window in Anne's room gives onto the back of the hotel, onto an empty courtyard where half a dozen cats lie sunning themselves—although late October and the days are getting shorter, darker. Right away Anne plans to visit museums, churches, cathedrals, but her first day in Paris she can hardly get out of bed. When finally she does, she stands at the window and watches the cats. She does not feel depressed so much as absent. She does not think about her husband, George, or about her daughters—what they might be doing. The only explanation, which was not an explanation Anne gave before she left, was that the two girls were old enough to look after themselves and that George would just have to cope with the groceries, the cooking, the washing and whatever Anne did all day. Making a vague fanning motion with her hand, Anne told George she needed air.

The second day Anne rouses herself and walks from Sainte-Chapelle, to Notre-Dame, to the Louvre; the third day it rains and Anne buys a lot of expensive clothes: a dress, a suede jacket, a pair of trousers, two silk blouses; she charges them to George. She also starts to feel lonely. (Except for the man sitting at the next table in a restaurant who asks Anne if she recommends her *canard à l'orange*—not looking up from the magazine she is reading, Anne answers a barely audible *oui*—Anne has spoken to no one except to salespersons and waiters.) On the fourth day, a man follows Anne as she walks along the quays back to the hotel. Although her heart is pounding and she wants to run, she remembers a stupid joke she once heard about an American tourist who, instead of calling the man on the *métro* who pinches her *cochon*—pig—tells him *couchons*—let's sleep together. Two hours later, when Anne leaves the hotel again to have dinner, the man is across the street, smoking a cigarette, waiting for her. *Couchons!*

Standing at her window the next morning, looking down at the cats in the courtyard—by then, Anne has a favorite, a big marmalade cat who, except for an occasional impatient flick of his tail, lies motionless for hours—she decides to call her school friend Nina.

At the Montpellier train station, Anne, her large suitcase at her feet, waits for Nina. As usual Nina is late, and Anne is reminded of all the times Nina has kept her waiting—in particular, the time that led to her meeting George, since she could not keep saving the seat at the sold-out Stéphane Grappelli concert for Nina indefinitely. At last Anne sees Nina.

"You look just the same," Anne says, kissing Nina, who is thinner. Her hair is streaked with gray.

"So do you," Nina answers breathlessly. "Always *très* chic."

In college, both Anne and Nina majored in French; after graduation, Nina went abroad to study music and fell in love with a musician.

Anne shakes her head; suddenly she feels like crying. "Your children?" she asks instead.

"At home, with Michel." Michel, the musician, is already married to someone else, to a woman named Eliane, whom he cannot divorce; Nina and Michel have two small children, a girl and a boy. "Here, let me." Nina reaches for Anne's suitcase.

Embarrassed all of a sudden by the size and the weight of the suitcase, Anne hands Nina her new jacket instead. "Take this," she says.

"Oh, how beautiful." Nina strokes the suede. "I'll have to borrow it from you," she says, smiling. They both know that Nina is referring to the many times in college when Nina borrowed Anne's clothes. Often, without asking.

"No, keep it," Anne says. "I mean it," she adds.

As Anne opens the door to Nina's car, a large white dog lying on the front seat raises its head.

"Get, July! Get in the back," Nina tells the dog. "She followed us from the beach last summer—the children insisted on keeping her. But don't go near her, she sheds." The backseat of Nina's car is littered with toys, a discarded sweater, a child's sandal, food wrappers. "Don't mind the mess," Nina also says.

In addition to borrowing Anne's clothes in college, Nina was incapable of putting her own clothes away. She left everything trailing on chairs or lying on the floor. But it was her sweetness more than anything else that attracted Anne, and Nina's selflessness—she had a kind of otherworldliness, a total lack of ego, is how Anne always described her.

*   *   *

"How many people live in however you pronounce the name of your village?" Anne asks as Nina starts up the car. The village is a few miles north of Montpellier.

"St. Guilhem-le-Désert," Nina enunciates the name for Anne. "About two hundred, except on weekends and holidays, then it is more like two million people, who come here to climb the Cévennes. Also, you would be surprised at the number of pilgrims."

"Pilgrims?"

"Yes, they come to worship a three-inch piece of the True Cross, which Charlemagne is said to have given to one of his favorite knights, a man named Guilhem who built an abbey. You can visit it if you like. Now a community of Carmelite nuns lives—Oh, I don't mean to go on about the local sights." Nina reaches with one hand to touch Anne's arm. "Tell me," she says, "how's George?"

"I think I've left him," Anne answers, turning to look out of the side window so that Nina cannot see her face. "Nothing is settled yet. But go on, I like hearing about where you live."

"There's a castle. We can visit that too," Nina tells Anne after a while.

"Oh, what a pretty house!" Anne exclaims as Nina parks the car. "It looks as if it was built back in the Middle Ages."

"It was." Nina laughs. "There's practically no heat in winter and there's just enough hot water to fill a teakettle."

"I'm so happy to see you," Anne says, getting out of the car and brushing at her skirt, which is covered with dog hair.

Nina's children, Sophie and Paul, are sitting at the kitchen table coloring in a book. Michel, a big man in a red wool checked shirt, sits with them. He has on a headset and is listening to music; he does not hear Nina and Anne come in.

"Hello, *chéri*!" Nina shouts.

Anne stands at the door and smiles at the children, who are staring at her. July, the dog, trots past her and Sophie gets down from the chair and, kneeling, puts her arms around the dog's neck.

"*Je t'aime*," she croons.

Looking up, Michel turns off the music and takes off his headset.

Her hand extended, Anne walks up to him. "Nice to meet you, Michel."

"How was your trip, Anne?" he asks, his English is heavily accented. Then, turning to the children, Michel says, "Anne, here, went to school with *maman* when *maman* was a girl." Michel speaks as if this is the first time Anne's name has ever been mentioned. "She lives in America, don't you, Anne?"

Anne nods.

"Come, let me show you to your room," Nina says.

Anne's room is Sophie's, and Sophie has been moved into Paul's room. The bed is a narrow child's bed, and the quilt is covered with faded figures of Babar. Once Nina has gone back downstairs, Anne sets her suitcase at the foot of the bed and opens it; all her clothes—sweaters, skirts, jackets—are carefully wrapped in tissue to keep them from wrinkling. There is no closet in the room, only a few hangers dangle from a hook on the back of the door, and Anne decides not to unpack after all. Instead she takes out her flowered toilet kit and goes down the hall to the only bathroom. When she tries to lock the bathroom door, she finds that the lock does not turn.

In the afternoon, Michel leaves to play in his band in Montpellier, and Nina drives Sophie to a ballet lesson. Anne stays with Paul, who has turned on an old black-and-white television set to watch cartoons. The picture has a grainy quality she remembers from her own childhood.

* * *

When Anne wakes up it takes her a few seconds to re-member where she is. "Paul?" she asks.

"He's here, he's fine." Nina says, standing in the doorway. "You fell asleep."

Apparently, while she was sleeping, Paul went out-side to pile stones on the side of the road. "I can't believe I did that," Anne says.

"Don't worry about it," Nina tells her. "As the young-est, Paul has a highly developed sense of self-preservation, and there's never much traffic on our street. Look how perfectly this fits me," she says, changing the subject and twirling around in Anne's suede jacket. Then, remember-ing dinner, Nina says, "You must be starving, Anne. And I told you, didn't I, that Michel is a vegetarian?"

"Do you have anything to drink?" Anne asks Nina, who is boiling water for spaghetti. "Wine?"

"Wine? Oh, I'm sorry. I'll ask Michel to get some tomorrow."

"It doesn't matter. I just thought if you did . . . Here," Anne also says, "let me do something useful."

As Anne is setting the table she can hear Nina hum-ming in the kitchen. Nina had a beautiful singing voice. When she sang, everyone said, Nina was transformed. She became powerful, important.

Although fairly sure of the answer, Anne calls out to Nina in the next room, "Are you still singing?"

*   *   *

In bed, that night, underneath the flimsy Babar quilt, Anne keeps all her clothes on—except for her shoes—the room is so damp and cold. Disoriented and uncomfortable, she does not sleep much. She hears Michel come up the stairs—by the luminous hands on her watch, which she has not bothered to change, it is ten o'clock in the evening on the East Coast of the United States—and for a moment she confuses him with George, about whom she has been dreaming. (In the dream, she is in a crowded room, at a party perhaps, where George, who does not smoke, is smoking and offering everyone at the party a cigarette—a special blend, George keeps repeating in a boastful and unfamiliar way.) Later, at seven and while it is still dark, she hears Nina get the children ready for school. Anne waits until she hears Nina drive off, then she gets up and dresses—she merely puts on another sweater and brushes her hair. On her way downstairs, she stops off at the bathroom. Wearing the red checked shirt, Michel is sitting on the toilet, reading a magazine.

"Oh!" Embarrassed, Anne quickly shuts the bathroom door.

Barely glancing up, Michel says, "*Pas de problème.*"

*   *   *

"How about a walk?" Nina suggests when she returns. "We can go up to the castle, but it's a bit of a hike. I'll take July—it will be good exercise for her."

Rue du Bout-du-Monde—End-of-the-World Road, Nina translates for Anne. A steep and narrow road, and Anne is grateful that she has on her walking shoes. Even so, she slips on the loose stones and pebbles. On either side of her, the ground is covered with mostly impenetrable scrub and oak thickets.

"Michel took me up here when we first met. I didn't notice how steep it was then," Nina says with a little laugh. She has July on a leash and the dog is pulling her.

"Perfect if you're a goat," Anne says.

"Or a sheep. In summer, the place is filled with them. Each year the shepherds bring up their flocks. You should see all the lambs—" Nina stops. "But I'd rather hear about you, Anne."

"The two girls are all right," Anne begins in an expressionless voice. "They're in school, they're getting good grades, they've already decided on careers: Danielle wants to be a doctor, Joyce a lawyer."

"And George? Is there someone else?"

Anne shakes her head. "Sometimes, I wish there was. There's nothing I can really point my finger at. It's just . . ." She hesitates. "It's just so trivial and predictable. And I guess it always boils down to the same thing—sex, which in our case is nearly nonexistent. I know, I know, I am being incredibly spoiled, but I want more and I want it to be different."

"Different is not necessarily better," Nina says.

They walk on in silence—except for Nina occasionally telling July to stop or to heel—until they reach the top of the ridge and the castle. All that remains of it is the curtain wall and the sixty-foot-high keep faced with huge limestone blocks, but it is the view that draws them. The sheer drop from the cliff and the gorge hundreds of feet below.

"So what happened to Guilhem?" Anne asks.

"After his wife died, Guilhem gave up all his worldly possessions and became a monk. He spent the rest of his life in a cell, fasting, praying—" Far down in the village, a church bell begins to ring the hour—eleven o'clock. "And according to the legend," Nina continues, "when Guilhem died, all the church bells began to ring at once of their own accord without anyone pulling on the ropes."

Again, that night, Michel leaves to play in the band, but at dinner Nina holds up a bottle of wine. She pours Anne a glass, then herself a glass as well. "I know it's funny," she says. "Most people, including my family, think that musicians drink, smoke and are completely dissipated, but Michel isn't like that. And he's a wonderful father."

Anne takes a sip of wine. "So, you're really happy, Nina?"

Nina shrugs. "Happy? Sure, I'm happy. I miss a lot of things. I wish Michel did not have to struggle so hard to get work. But I love him and I love the children."

Except to say good morning and good-bye and making sure to knock before she uses the bathroom, Anne has barely spoken to Michel. "You don't mind not being married?"

"I don't think about it anymore. And, in a funny way, I like Eliane. Sophie and Paul like her, too."

That night, Anne cannot go to sleep, but instead of tossing and turning under the flimsy Babar quilt, she turns on the light and reads in a guidebook how first Guilhem captured the city of Nîmes by hiding his soldiers in wine barrels, then how he lost the tip of his nose fighting off the pagans in Rome. Hours later, Anne wakes up to find the light on in her room and, after a moment of confusion, to the sounds of Michel and Nina making love. *Couchons!* Anne is reminded of the man who followed her in Paris—he was not bad-looking in a foreign sort of way. It would have been easy.

*   *   *

"What kind of music do you play?" Anne asks Michel in the morning. Nina is taking the children to school, and Michel is making coffee in the kitchen. "Rock?"

Michel nods. "And whatever people want to hear. Would you like some coffee, Anne?"

"I'd love to hear you play," Anne goes on, handing Michel her cup. "Maybe, one of these nights I can go with Nina. My husband—you should meet him," she hears herself say, "he's a great music . . ." Anne's voice trails off—how to explain the word *fan*?

When Nina gets back to the house, she has a headache, the start of migraine, she says.

"I hope it wasn't the wine," Anne says.

Nina shakes her head. "I'll be fine later." She smiles at Anne but her eyes look watery and unfocused. "I just need some sleep," she says.

"Don't worry about me, Nina. I'll go for a walk," Anne says. "Oh, can I get you something? Tea?" she adds too late—Nina is halfway up the stairs and does not hear her.

"You can walk to the Grotte de Clamouse," Michel tells Anne after Nina has left.

"The *grotte*? Is it a cave?"

Michel nods. "It's three kilometers from here. I can start you on your way, if you like. Show you a shortcut, so you won't have to walk on the main road."

"That's very kind of you," Anne answers. "I'll go and put on my walking shoes."

When Anne comes back, Michel, too, has changed. He is wearing a different shirt, a clean white cotton one.

"Some of the caves are so far underground they have never seen the light of day, yet bunches of green ferns grow inside them," Michel tells Anne as they set off through the village. Michel walks fast and Anne has to nearly run to keep up with him. "You can see beautiful crystals in the shape of flowers," he says. "Bouquets of flowers made from pure white aragonite."

"*Aragoneat?*" Anne repeats after him, mimicking his pronunciation. She feels stupid. She knows nothing about caves or crystals.

"My father often worked as a guide, he took tourists to visit the caves. He also had the good fortune to go on several exploratory expeditions with Martel." When Anne does not answer, Michel continues, "Édouard-Alfred Martel, the famous how do you say, *spéléogiste.*"

"Ah, yes. *Spéléogiste.*" Anne feels as if she was having a conversation with someone from another planet; uncharacteristically, she is tempted to laugh. She bends her head so that Michel cannot see her while she tries to compose her face. After a while, so as to say something, she asks, "Your father is from this region? This *région?*" Anne repeats it the French way.

They have reached the outskirts of the village and instead of answering her, Michel points out a path that runs parallel to the main road. "One of the oldest *transhumance* in the Cévennes begins right here. When I was a boy I went every summer with my father when he took up the *ships.*"

Again, Anne is tempted to laugh.

"Yes. Sheep, Nina told me how—" she starts to say when, without warning, Michel takes her in his arms and tries to kiss her on the mouth. Letting out a cry of surprise, Anne shakes herself free of him.

Anne has tied a scarf around her head. Now the ends of the scarf whip around and hit her face, startling her. The day, which started out mild, has turned chilly, and the wind has picked up. Fast-moving clouds hide the sun; any moment it looks as if it might rain. No one else is on the path, which, instead of running parallel to the road, winds more and more steeply up the hillside, who knows to where? And who would find her if she twists an ankle or breaks a leg? There are no signs or markers, and Anne is angry with herself for taking Michel's advice and not walking on the road instead. Also, she is angry at Michel. Fool, she thinks, not sure whom she means. Then she stops so abruptly she almost loses her balance. She was about to step on something that she does not immediately identify—a mass of dirty white wool.

A year to the day after Anne leaves St. Guilhem-le-Désert, Nina dies of a brain tumor—the cause of the headaches, Anne supposes. Michel telephones at two o'clock one morning—eight o'clock in St. Guilhem-le-Désert—to let her know, and it takes Anne, who is in bed asleep next to George, a while to understand who Michel is and what he is telling her. "What time is it there?" she asks foolishly, at the same time that, in the background, she hears the bells begin to ring. The St. Guilhem-le-Désert church bells. Next, still only half awake, Anne asks Michel if there is anything she can do for him or the children. "I am going to go back and live with my wife, Eliane," Michel says. "Perhaps this time we can work it out."

The dead sheep was lying right across her path. Underneath the matted wool, Anne could see a row of startlingly white rib bones, and underneath the rib bones, the ground. The sheep must have been dead for quite some time. Anne had to step over the dead sheep and continue on the path or else go back down.

My Music

The only song my father, who could not sing, sang was one he learned while he was in the French Foreign Legion. He sang it with his fellow legionnaires as he marched in North Africa during World War II. The brisk pace and repetitive lyrics roused his spirits and helped him endure the oppressive heat of the Sahara Desert.

> *Auprès de ma blonde,*
> *Qu'il fait bon, fait bon, fait bon.*
> *Auprès de ma blonde,*
> *Qu'il fait bon dormir*

Later, my father claimed that his time in the Foreign Legion was one of the happiest in his life. He reminisced about drinking the cheap yet good Algerian wine and his friendship with Josephine Baker—a lifelong one, as it turned out—whose lover was also a legionnaire. Later, too, when he tried to sing "Auprès de Ma Blonde" to my mother, who was in fact blonde and beautiful, she did not pay the song or my father much attention.

Briefly, when I was seven years old and living in Paris—a gray Paris, suffering the deprivations and food shortages that resulted from the war—twice a week I had piano lessons. I don't remember very much about those lessons except that I learned how to play the scales and read a little music because soon, my teacher, whose name I long ago forgot, in her blunt French way told my parents that they were wasting their money and, she, her time. Instead, the person I remember best from that period was the one-armed elevator man at the Hotel Raphaël, where my parents and I were staying temporarily, whom my parents had engaged to walk me to school every morning. Maurice was a thin, dignified, gentle man who had lost an arm in the First World War and who always wore his high-collared, gold trimmed, hotel uniform, the empty sleeve neatly tucked inside the pocket. As we walked together down avenue Kléber, where the hotel was situated, past the Trocadero and up avenue Georges Mandel, where my school, Les Abeilles, was located—I holding his one hand—Maurice taught me to sing:

Malbrouk s'en va-t-en guerre,
Mironton, mironton, mirontaine.

A few years later, when I was living in America, and during my school holidays, I was sent to visit my stern German-born grandmother. Determined to improve me, she set herself the thankless task of giving me a classical music education. For an hour every afternoon, she had me sit in the modest living room of her Cayuga Heights apartment in Ithaca, New York—in Bonn, where she was from, her house had been destroyed by Allied bombing—and listen to the local classical radio station. An hour that dragged into an eternity; outside the sun was shining and I could hear the boys in the fraternity house across the street getting ready for another party. But one afternoon turned out to be different. I was listening to Beethoven's *Fidelio* (my grandmother had outlined the plot and told me to listen for the sound of trumpets, which would signal Fidelio's release from prison) and, to this day, I can recall the feeling of accomplishment and of triumph—especially of triumph—when I heard those trumpets.

In college, where I was delinquent in all my studies, I spent my time either in Boston taking ballet lessons

—I had a sudden and unjustified desire to become a ballerina—or lying on my unmade bed, listening to records. I loved Adolphe Adam's *Giselle,* for obvious reasons; Renata Tebaldi singing arias brought hot passionate tears to my eyes and furious banging at my door: "Turn the damn music down!"; Elaine Stritch singing "The Saga of Jenny" was another favorite, as was the English musical *Salad Days*; and I especially cherished a scratched recording of Noël Coward's reedy voice singing "Someday I'll Find You."

While he was courting me, my former husband, who prided himself on his voice, which indeed was good, used to sing a song about how anything could happen on a "lazy, dazy, golden" afternoon. I had never heard the song before nor have I since, but for a short while then I fancied I would be the one to fill the nebulous and abstract role of *anything*, which in my mind translated itself into *love, happiness* and *a marriage*, all of which it did for a bit. For a bit, too, we lived in a large, elegant house in Charlottesville, Virginia, which had once belonged to my husband's aunt. Along with the house, we had inherited her piano, a Bechstein. His aunt, a glamorous and charming woman, had been married to a Russian prince—one of the princes who unsuccessfully tried to kill Rasputin—and had lived in Paris. Among her many acquaintances—Colette, Coco Chanel, other exiled Russian princes—was Arthur Rubinstein, who, according to one of her stories, at lunch one day, announced that he was going to a Bechstein auction to buy a piano. "Of course, Arthur dear, you must buy yourself the very best piano," said the aunt, "but will you buy me the second best?" A few days later, a piano was delivered to the aunt's avenue Foch apartment—it was hauled up through the window—and a few weeks later, Arthur Rubinstein himself came to lunch again. After lunch, the aunt asked him to play something on her new Bechstein and Arthur Rubinstein sat at the piano and began to play a Bach prelude but, after only a few minutes, he banged down on the keys and abruptly stopped. "Arthur, Arthur, what is wrong?" cried the aunt and Arthur Rubinstein answered, "I bought you the very best piano." Once a year, at great expense, I hired a piano tuner who came all the way down from Richmond to tune the "best" Bechstein. No one, except for an occasional guest, ever played the piano and, to compensate, the piano tuner suggested that I run my thumb down all the keys once a day. I tried to do this a few times but the ivory keys hurt my thumb and mostly I was too busy raising three small children.

*   *   *

I used to joke—only it was partly true—that if I could have only one wish, I would wish that I could sing. To this day, I would wish the same thing. What a pleasure and what a gift, I think, it must be to open one's mouth and have a beautiful song effortlessly come out. Unfortunately, I cannot carry a tune. Nevertheless, when my children were small, to put them to sleep, I sang to them in French:

> *Il était un petit navire,*
> *Qui n'avait ja-ja jamais navigué,*

or my favorite, the less soothing:

> *Malbrouk s'en va-t-en guerre,*
> *Mironton, mironton, mirontaine,*
> *Ne sait quand reviendra,*
> *Ne sait quand reviendra.*

Thanks to Maurice, I still knew the lyrics and I also knew the reason Malbrouk's wife was waiting for him in vain:

> *Monsieur Malbrouk est mort,*
> *Mironton, mironton, mirontaine,*
> *Monsieur Malbrouk est mort,*
> *Est mort et enterré.*

The reason, too, I sang to my children in French was I believed that anyone who might be listening to me—including my then husband—knew neither French nor the songs and therefore would not know whether I was singing off-key, which chances are I was.

One of my favorite paintings is *Rest During the Flight to Egypt,* by Caravaggio. At the center of the picture, an angel, his back to the viewer, stands naked, except for a swirl of white cloth, his wings—wings as startlingly black as a crow's wings—gracefully outstretched. The angel is playing the violin for the Holy Family as they rest. Sitting on the ground, an attentive but weary-looking Joseph is holding up the sheet music for the angel to sight read while, next to him, Mary is holding the baby Jesus in her arms and both are asleep. The painting speaks to the power of music. This notion is taken a step further when, once a year, a concert is held in the Palazzo Doria Pamphilj, where the Caravaggio painting hangs, and the notes on the sheet music Joseph holds up to the angel are played.

My second husband also had a good voice, which makes me wonder whether I am drawn to musical men—and aren't opposites meant to attract? He loved to sing and he was clever at making up lyrics (in his heart, instead of being a lawyer, he wanted to write songs and be a lyricist). He loved Ira Gershwin, Richard Rodgers, Harold Arlen, Irving Berlin, he knew all the old show tunes by heart. The singer Carly Simon, too, was a favorite. Driving in the car, with his children, they all knew the words to her songs. Together they sang so well that, momentarily silenced and excluded, I was envious of them—of their talent and of their happiness at singing together.

When my husband died, I chose the music for his memorial service. For the prelude and the postlude, to be certain, I chose Bach; for hymns, I chose ones my husband had liked, "Love Divine" and "Jerusalem"; for myself, I chose Henry Purcell's *Music for the Funeral of Queen Mary,* the last part, the *canzona,* played by two trumpeters.

I spend the summers on an island in Maine and each summer, obsessively, I listen to a single CD: last summer it was Fabrizio De Andrè; the summer of 2006 it was Leonard Cohen; the summer of 2005 it was Mariza Nunes singing fado; the summer of 2004 it was the Pink Martini; K. D. Lang was in either 2003 or 2002, I forget; the year I did not listen to K. D. Lang, I listened to the soundtrack of Lars von Trier's movie *Breaking the*

Waves; the year before I listened to the Buena Vista Social Club. I am not a particularly sanguine person but when I listen to music, I can be transported. Also, I play the music as loud as I can and except for a bunch of seals, who at low tide lie not far away on an exposed reef, my nearest neighbor is a mile away. I listen to music at the end of the day, at sunset, and although my house faces east, I can watch the clouds turn from bright orange to pink and mauve, then purple streaked with gray—the colors reflecting on the water below them—and finally go dark; then, still to the sound of music, I can watch the moon rise.

The Riding Teacher

His obituary in the local paper said that Chingis was a quiet man who chose to live his life close to nature. The obituary also said that he was self-reliant and frugal and had built his house himself; that he carried water from a well; cooked on a woodstove and wasted nothing. He was a close observer of animals, especially of birds, and the birds, it said, came to eat out of his hand. The obituary also went on to say how he had once been a superb horseman and that he had founded a well-attended riding academy. He was born in 1925 in the Caucasus, he had never married nor did he have any known living relatives and it was a neighbor, who looked in on him from time to time and did some of his shopping, who discovered him—dead several days apparently, and the cause of death a heart attack most probably. The obituary concluded by saying that this quiet, gentle and reclusive man was a direct descendant of Genghis Khan.

Annette, a geneticist, now living in the Midwest and working for a pharmaceutical company, would never have seen the obituary except for the fact that she subscribes to a service on her computer that alerts her to any mention of the name "Genghis Khan." Her current research is based on a claim that 8 percent of the men living in the former Mongol empire, which translates into roughly sixteen million men, carry nearly identical Y chromosomes. Since, as Annette knows, the Y chromosome is passed on as a chunk of DNA from father to son, except for random mutations, it basically remains unchanged through generations and these random mutations, which occur naturally and are harmless, are called markers. Once these markers have been identified, Annette also knows, they must be traced back in time to the point at which they first occurred, thus determining the precise lineage of descent—as in the case of Genghis Khan, nearly a thousand years ago. Natural selection plays the dominant role in patterns of genetic variation and human population diversity, but in Genghis Khan's case, Annette is certain that the genetic mutations that have occurred are the result of the unique conditions— rape and slaughter—on which the Mongol empire was founded. However, to prove this, Annette must first have access to Genghis Khan's DNA or to the DNA of one of his male descendants.

All this time, Annette thinks, and she had no idea—nor had Lena—that Chingis was related to Genghis Khan. In fact, now that she is thinking about it, she remembers how, behind his ramrod-straight back, because he was so stern, so uncompromising, they had called him Genghis. And funny, too, how until now she had never made the connection—Chingis and Genghis are one and the same name. A strange irony, she thinks, but that is not exactly the right term for it. Coincidence is more apt, yet that is not quite right either. Annette settles for surprising and for looking back.

Two horse-crazy little girls, she and Lena were. She has a distinct picture of them at age nine or ten, galloping round and round on their parents' suburban lawns—they lived next door to each other—on their imaginary horses. Annette's horse was an Appaloosa, Lena's a more elegant five-gaited palomino. "Whoa, whoa," the girls said to themselves, pulling on the imaginary reins. "Whoa, there" as they slowed down to a trot. Later, they began to ride in earnest. First they rode at a local farm owned by two lesbians, Jill and Maureen, who boarded horses. Jill was an angry redhead—angry at the president of the country for raising taxes, angry at the postman for not delivering the mail on time, angry at Annette for not mucking out a stall properly. In addition to teaching the girls how to ride, Jill taught them how to care for horses, feed them, clean their tack, how, even, to shoe them. Annette can still see Jill, dressed in her heavy leather apron, holding a horse's leg firmly between her own, paring down the hoof with a knife that looked like a little scythe—as easy as trimming fingernails, Jill said, also pointing out the delicate frog inside the hoof. Maureen was pale and anorexic; she looked unwell and she rarely came outside. Annette could see her silhouette, her head bent, reading perhaps, through a window. Annette no longer remembers what happened in the end. Maureen may have died and Jill may have sold the farm and moved away. In any case, the two girls had already begun riding with Chingis.

Strange to think of him as old. And strange, too, that he never married. Or perhaps not so strange. What was the Russian saying she had once heard? A bachelor's life is a good life but he has a dog's death as no one is there to grieve for him, while a married man leads a dog's life but his death is pleasant as he is surrounded by his loved ones. Probably true for Chingis as well. Poor Chingis. He was so handsome, tall, dark, with almost impossibly high cheekbones and slightly slanted eyes—an adaptive advantage no doubt against the Siberian sleet and snow that harked back to his Mongol heritage—and always impeccably dressed in his khaki shirt and tie, jodhpurs, polished black riding boots and the captain's cap he wore. Unfailingly polite and correct to people, horses, dogs—some might have said humorless as well until one got to know him better—and remote, except, Annette imagines, to Lena.

Growing up, Annette and Lena spent almost every day on weekends and in summers—except for the one Lena and her family went to Greece and part of another when Annette had an emergency appendectomy—at Chingis's riding stable. They learned to jump, they learned a little dressage, they learned to ride green horses that bucked and shied. Tirelessly, Annette and Lena worked them in the ring—circling, changing leads, doing figure eights. Coordinated and supple, Lena was the more relaxed and, perhaps, the more fearless rider, while Annette was the more elegant rider.

They also went on long rides in what was then still open country, past cornfields and into cool woods of spreading beeches; they crossed clear streams, often pausing to let the horses drink. One time, on a particularly hot day, Annette and Lena tied up their horses and, taking off their clothes, went for a swim. When they looked up they saw Chingis who, on his own—or perhaps he had followed them—had ridden up to the bank of the stream. "I can either take your clothes and you will have to ride back naked," he teased them, laughing, "or I can take the horses and you will have to walk back—a long hot walk."

"I'll ride naked," Lena said.

More cautious, Annette said she preferred to walk.

Another time, Annette was cantering on a young mare when the mare put her foot in a gopher hole and fell. Annette went down underneath her, her foot caught in the stirrup. The mare got up before Annette could free her foot and by the time Chingis caught the mare by the reins, the mare was dragging Annette on the ground. Jumping off his horse, Chingis quickly freed Annette's foot from the stirrup. Then, leaning down, his face pale, he asked, "Are you hurt?"

"I don't think so." Annette shook her head.

Holding both horses's reins in one hand, Chingis helped Annette to her feet. He retrieved her hard hat, which had come off, brushed the dirt off her and watched as she put the hat back on. "Are you okay?" he asked again.

Not sure, Annette nodded. His concern, more than the fall, brought sudden tears to her eyes.

Chingis smiled, relieved. Then without another word, he gave Annette a leg up and she was back in the saddle on top of the fidgety mare.

Although himself a great rider, Genghis Khan's death was caused by a fall from a horse. He died a few days later, probably from the internal injuries he sustained from the fall. His body was brought back in a cart to his birthplace near Ulan Bator in Mongolia. By then, 1227, his empire extended across Asia, from the Pacific Ocean to the Caspian Sea. According to Genghis Khan's wishes, his death had to be kept secret. Thus, anyone unlucky enough to meet the funeral procession along the way was killed—innocent little children, pregnant women, old people, it made no difference who they were. Once Genghis Khan was buried, a herd of horses was made to gallop back and forth over the grave site in order to cover it up and hide any trace of it. A forest of trees was then planted in the area and soldiers were stationed there for several years and until the trees had grown sufficiently tall to completely conceal the actual spot. These strategies were so successful that, to this day, no one knows where Genghis Khan is buried.

Rarely did Chingis talk about his family. His father, he let slip once, had been killed by the Bolsheviks; his mother had died a few years after she and Chingis settled in America. How? When? To each other, Annette and Lena made up stories: how his father was brutally hacked to pieces by a disorderly band of Reds; how Chingis and his mother, a beautiful princess, escaped from Russia.

"His mother, " Lena told Annette, "wore a dress with pearl buttons down the front and as she and Chingis fled from the Bolsheviks, she was forced to give a pearl button to each person who had helped them."

More literal-minded, Annette shook her head. "You mean by the time Chingis and his mother reached America, her dress was undone?"

They speculated about his age—Chingis must be in his midthirties—his habits—he loved opera he once told them and he read a lot. Who were his favorite authors? Dickens? Eliot? Trollope? the Russian writers? Turgenev? Dostoyevsky and Tolstoy?

"Dostoyevsky!" Lena was ready to bet. "He's so dark," she said.

But mostly Annette and Lena speculated about his love life. They ran into him at the local movie theater one night—or rather they happened to sit several rows behind Chingis and a blonde woman. The woman had her hair up in a French twist and she wore a shawl—it looked like cashmere—over her shoulders. To Annette and Lena, she seemed sophisticated and probably she was from the city. Chingis had his arm around the back of the seat and it was difficult to tell, in the dark, if his arm was touching the woman's shoulders. They were also sharing a bag of popcorn, which surprised Annette and Lena—popcorn was so plebeian—yet occasionally their fingers must have touched inside the bag. Occasionally, too, during the movie, Chingis bent his head toward the woman and said something that made her laugh. The movie was a comedy but Annette and Lena hardly watched it.

Afterward, Annette and Lena debated whether they should mention seeing him.

"We could say, 'How did you like the movie, Chingis?'" Annette suggested.

"Or we could say, 'Who was the blonde babe you were with at the movies, Chingis?'" Lena said.

When they next saw Chingis, Annette and Lena said nothing.

Lena's parents were Greek and she had inherited their Mediterranean olive complexion and dark, thick curly hair. Her eyebrows, too, were thick and black, nearly meeting in the middle. A little scar ran through one eyebrow and the hairs there had turned white, which added a slight but not unappealing distraction to her face. She had a small Byzantine nose that came straight down from her brow, large dark eyes and a wide mouth. She laughed a lot and her teeth were startlingly straight and white. She was small; her body strong and compact—she could have been a gymnast. Annette was tall, blonde, first scrawny then thin—very different from Lena.

> Genghis Khan began his conquests by uniting the disparate Mongol tribes—the Merkits, Naimans, Kerats, Tatars, Uyghurs—and establishing a single military force under his leadership. He was a brilliant and charismatic chieftain as well as a violent and cruel one. His success was attributed to his extensive network of spies and the psychological impact caused by his methods—the total destructions of cities, the murder and rape of its citizens. He is reported to have once boasted: "The greatest happiness is to vanquish your enemies, to chase them before you, to rob them of their wealth, to see those dear to them bathed in tears, to clasp to your bosom their wives and daughters." Fear was his most useful tactic. He was also known never to shirk personal danger or hardship. On the war trail, along with his fellow soldiers, Genghis slept and ate as they did, subsisting on yak milk and, occasionally, to fortify himself, opening up a horse's vein and drinking the blood.

Chingis's house was across the street from the stables. A small, white two-story shingle house with a gable roof. On the few occasions Annette had been inside—to fetch something, to make a phone call—the house was always tidy. Immaculate. The kitchen, too. Shiny copper pots and pans hung from hooks above the stove; the dish towels and pot holders were neatly folded on the counter; a glass, a dish or a fork left to dry in the rack was the only visible sign that someone might have eaten there. Neatly stacked books and records and an old-fashioned bulky record player filled the living room; the sofa and chairs were covered with old horse quilts and blankets—protection no doubt against the two or three dogs who invariably shared the house. In the front hall, along the wall, were framed photographs of Chingis's family and Annette always paused to look at Chingis's father in riding breeches and boots, wearing a tall fur hat and holding a whip; in another photo, Chingis's father was on horseback, jumping onto what looked to be the roof of a house; a photograph of his mother showed a handsome, dark-haired woman, wearing an elaborate headdress. There was one photo of Chingis in his army uniform looking young and untroubled. Although Annette never went so far as to go upstairs in Chingis's house—she was tempted but never quite dared—nowhere was there any sign, as far as she could tell, of a "blonde babe."

In addition to the dogs—mixed breeds, strays or ones from the local pound—Chingis kept chickens. The chickens were a rare breed from the Far East and they had long glossy, black tail feathers and were not friendly. In particular, the rooster, who had several spurs on each leg and who made as if to attack if anyone approached the coop. According to Chingis, the most unusual thing about the rooster was that he was said to have black bones. Also he could fly. Chingis was inordinately proud of his chickens and although they rarely laid eggs, he made a big show of giving an egg away if one did.

The eggs were small and nasty. They had specks of blood in them—the chick embryo—and Lena and Annette, rather than bring them home or eat them, threw the eggs out.

But perhaps because chickens were ultimately connected to food and to cooking, a predominantly female occupation, it was a subject Annette felt free to joke with him about.

"So, Chingis," she asked, "how many eggs did you get this week? Enough for an omelette?"

Chingis, too, did not mind the banter and responded in kind, "Not an omelette, Annette—a soufflé."

The summer Annette and Lena graduated from high school, and the summer before they each were going to go away to college, to different colleges—Annette already knew she wanted to study medicine, unsure Lena was going to a liberal arts college—was also the summer that Annette got appendicitis. Worse, her appendix burst and she got peritonitis. According to the doctor, Annette easily could have died. As a result, she had to spend a month recuperating and could not ride. Toward the end of the month, when she felt nearly well, Annette would drive to the stable in the morning with Lena and help out with some of the chores. She brought in the horses from the pasture, she fed and watered them, she helped saddle them up for the young riders taking lessons. All the same, Annette sensed that things had changed. Both Lena and Chingis—although initially pleased to see her recovered and grateful for her help— seemed oblivious of her. They joked and were noisy. They acted foolish, almost. Especially Chingis. Inside a horses's stall, Annette caught him humming a tune.

"A Russian song. A Russian love song," Chingis volunteered, putting his arms in a mock embrace around the horse's neck and smiling.

Annette had to ask, "Lena, is something going on with you and Chingis?"

At first, Lena denied it. Uncharacteristically, she was blushing. "You can't say anything. Or tell anyone," she finally admitted.

"I won't," Annette promised.

It began, Lena told Annette, on the way back from the hospital after they had first visited Annette. "You were so doped up, you probably don't remember," Lena also said. "He drove me home—well, not right away, first we went and got a beer."

"Then?" Annette pressed. She was genuinely surprised. She also felt hurt or, more accurately, betrayed.

"I'm in love with him," Lena said. She looked away. "If my parents find out, they'll kill me," she also said.

"You're sleeping with him?" Annette asked.

"Don't," Lena said, by way of an answer.

Even after Annette started to ride again, things were not the same. She avoided Chingis, she avoided Lena. Her excuse was to give them time alone together but she also suddenly felt uncomfortable and disoriented in their presence. The way Chingis stood next to Lena's horse, stroking the horse's neck and looking up at her. The way Lena laughed down at him, flicking him lightly with her crop. The way he touched her knee. How happy and handsome he looked. It all made Annette feel diminished. Envious. Toward the end of August, she stopped riding. She had to get ready for college, she told Lena.

Instead of coming home, Annette spent Thanksgiving in California with her roommate's parents in nearby San Luis Obispo. She did, however, come home at Christmas. She arrived just in time as the next day, a heavy snowstorm blanketed most of New England. The power went out and it took several days before the roads were sufficiently plowed out and before Annette and Lena could safely drive to the stables and ride. On the way over, Annette asked Lena, "Are you still seeing Chingis?"

Lena nodded. "It's hard. He wants me to quit college and get married."

"Get married?" Annette echoed, shocked.

On account of the weather, they had to ride indoors. Chingis stood in the middle of the ring shouting out instructions. Again, he had changed—a dark shadow had crossed his face—and nothing the two girls did pleased him. Impatient, he cracked his whip and made the horses tense and nervous. Outside the wind rattled the flimsy windows of the indoor ring and that, too, made the horses nervous. He picked on Lena.

"How many times do I have to tell you not to shift your weight? Leg pressure is enough." He sounded angry.

Lena, too, was angry. "Give me a break, Genghis," she muttered under her breath so he could not hear.

"What did you say, Lena? Speak up." Chingis taunted her.

"Go to hell," Lena said, getting off her horse and running out of the ring. She was crying.

"Lena!" Grabbing her horse's reins, Chingis ran after her.

For close to an hour, Annette trotted and cantered by herself. Dutifully, she did figure eights, she changed leads, until Chingis and Lena came back. Chingis was holding Lena's horse and he had his other arm around her shoulder. They both looked flushed. Neither Chingis nor Lena explained or apologized for their absence to Annette and she did not ask.

At Easter, again Annette chose to stay in California —her workload, she claimed. Also, she had started dating a boy named Robin. Once or twice, she tried to call Lena. The first time the person who answered the dorm telephone could not locate her—Lena was not in her room—the second time, the person—a different one this time—left the phone dangling from the hook for such a long time that eventually Annette was the one to hang up. Annette's parents, when she had inquired after Lena, told her that they had seen her a few times. Not surprising, her college was nearby and Lena often came home on weekends. Once Annette's parents spoke of how they had seen Lena getting in the car—she was wearing chaps and boots, clearly she was going riding. Another time, they mentioned how Lena had been involved in a slight accident—nothing serious and she was not injured, Annette's parents reassured her: the car had gone off the road, missing a tree and into a ditch. Perhaps, they hinted knowingly, Lena had been drinking.

Summer came and nearly went before Annette returned home again. She had gotten a job in San Luis

Obispo at a veterinary clinic, holding down dogs and cats and other small animals while they were being examined or getting their shots. She was still seeing Robin but she was also seeing Mark, one of the vets at the clinic. Mark was older and divorced and she was flattered by his attention and impressed by his expertise. She watched him put a skin-and-bones-thin whippet to sleep and was touched by how he spoke to the owner, an older woman, and, how together, they had held the dog. "Tell me when you are ready," Mark told her as if he, Mark, had all day. Also, Mark was an excellent horseback rider. At last, in late August, Annette went back home but Lena was not there.

As soon as she could, Annette drove out to Chingis's stables. Looking unchanged in his polished black riding boots, khaki shirt and cap, he stood in the middle of the ring, teaching a class of children how to post. When he saw Annette, he hurried over to her.

"Thank god, you're back," he said. "Do you know where she is?"

"Who? Lena?"

"Yes, Lena."

"No, I have no idea. On the phone last night, her mother said she was in New Hampshire. She got a job babysitting for the summer."

"Babysitting. Bullshit," Chingis scoffed.

The riding lesson finished, Chingis and Annette went inside the house. On the way, Annette noticed that the chicken coop was empty. "What happened to your chickens, Chingis?" she asked.

Chingis shrugged. "I gave them away. I've no time for chickens."

"I never did like the eggs," Annette tried to make light of the subject but Chingis did not answer her.

Shooing away the dogs that were lying on the living room sofa and chairs and shaking out the blankets so Annette could sit down, Chingis looked at his watch and asked, "Would you like some coffee?"

"Yes, thank you. Coffee would be great," Annette answered and waited for Chingis to speak.

Lena, Chingis said, was pregnant. He had begged her to marry him but, although she claimed to love him, she could not make up her mind. She was afraid of what her parents would say—she was nineteen, too young. Then Chingis told her she should get an abortion and after considerable discussion, arguments, tears, Lena agreed. Together, they made an appointment at the clinic—the first time, Lena canceled the appointment saying she had midterm exams, the second time she made up another excuse—and when finally they went, three weeks or so later, the doctor said it was too late. Lena was in her fourth month, she had waited too long.

Chingis was sitting across from Annette on the sofa. He put his head in his hands.

"She's so tiny but it barely showed. No one knew she was pregnant," he said.

"I had no idea," Annette said.

"She kept on riding. I told her she was crazy." Chingis looked at his watch. "I have another class in a few minutes. Anyway, her parents did find out eventually. Lena said they threatened to come and shoot me." Again, Chingis put his head in his hands. "They sent her away. To an aunt. She is due any day now. Then she will give the baby up for adoption."

Annette could not think of what to say. "Do you speak to her?"

"I did for a while. Now, she doesn't want to talk to me anymore. I don't know." Again, Chingis looked at his watch, then out the window as a car full of children drove up. "I've got to go, Annette." Abruptly, Chingis stood up. "Maybe you could try and call her. Find out how she is and find out about the baby."

"I'll try," Annette promised.

Annette finished her coffee. As usual, everything was tidy and in place in Chingis's kitchen. Putting her cup in the sink, Annette stood up and started to leave. Out the window, she could see him walking into the stable, followed by a bunch of children. On an impulse, she went upstairs. Tiptoeing into Chingis's bedroom, she was momentarily startled by a dog jumping off the bed. The bed was an old-fashioned four-poster, neatly made up. Lena, she thought. Lena and Chingis, naked, making love. Across from the bed, on top of the bureau, there was an old-fashioned ornate silver-backed set of hair and clothes brushes, a comb and hand mirror, which, Annette guessed, had belonged to Chingis's mother. Also a framed photograph of Lena, which Annette recognized right away as her high school graduation picture. The photograph did not do Lena justice. The photo made Annette inexplicably sad.

Several years went by before Annette saw Lena again. During that time, she occasionally received bits of news: Lena had gone to work on a dude ranch in Montana, Lena had joined an artist colony on the island of Ibiza in Spain, Lena was living in a commune in Kathmandu—never anything about a baby—while Annette, herself, went to medical school at Stanford, then she did a residency in a hospital in Ohio. When finally Annette came home it was to get married and Lena, then, too, was home.

She was much changed and had Annette met her in the street, she would not have recognized her—only she would not have met her in the street as Lena could hardly get out of bed. She has lost weight, her arms and legs were like sticks. Her skin was yellow, her large dark

he stood in line for the buffet and then as he sat by himself at a table eating a piece of wedding cake. A few times she saw him on the dance floor. Also, briefly, they danced together—before Annette's husband cut in—and Chingis had just time enough to tell Annette, "One day, I will find her."

At the time, she thought he meant Lena.

Pérou

The year is 1940 and I lie fast asleep under a fur blanket in a Balmoral pram. The midnight navy Silver Cross pram, with its reversible folding hood and hand-sprung chassis, glides smoothly and silently down rue Raynouard. (Until recently, I thought rue Raynouard, located in the Sixteenth Arrondissement in the area of Paris known as Passy—as the names sound almost exactly alike—was named after the painter and spelled *Renoir*. Instead the street is named after a dull French Academician, François-Juste-Marie Raynouard.) Jeanne, my nurse, pushes the pram. Over her heavily starched white uniform, she wears a blue wool coat that is nearly the same midnight navy as the pram and that reaches unstylishly to her midcalf. She also wears thick cotton stockings, a pair of white lace-up shoes and a coif. The coif, again the same matching navy blue, is secured to her forehead by a white bandeau and entirely covers her hair. Jeanne is pale, plain and nearsighted. She wears glasses and, if ever I catch a glimpse of her without them, it takes me a moment to readjust to her face. Jeanne, whose last name I don't remember or, worse, never knew since to me she was always simply *Jeanne,* comes from a village in Brittany. She is nineteen years old and will devote five years of her life to looking after me—years she will spend in Peru.

Peru of all unimaginable places!

Jeanne, we have to leave Paris. Leave France, is what I imagine my mother says to her.

You'll have to get a passport. A visa.

Oui, madame.

Does she have a choice?

Could she instead say *Non, madame?* I have to go back to *mon pays,* to *ma famille.*

A large family: the men fishermen, the women uncomplaining, hardworking. Mother, father, grandparents, aunts, uncles, brothers, sisters and cousins.

Peru? Since her grandparents went to Mont-Saint-Michel on their honeymoon fifty years ago, neither has traveled farther than the city of Brest. As far as they are concerned, Jeanne has disappeared off the face of the earth.

Where in God's name is that? Again and again Jeanne's father, a large man with an appetite for food and life, asks his wife, Jeanne's mother, Marie-Pauline. But, in the end, he looks it up for himself in one of the children's school atlases and he sees how far away Peru is from Brittany. He shakes his head sadly; in his heart, he knows he will not see Jeanne again.

Pérou, Annick, Jeanne's sister and the prettiest, says with a huge sigh. How I envy her. I would do anything to get away from this boring, stupid place. And, in a few months time, on a warm summer morning, wearing her best dress, a sleeveless, red-and-white flower print, and, bicycling quickly, without giving the village a single backward glance, she does.

What is Jeanne thinking? Handsome, blond Daniel and the cleverest of her brothers, thinks.

Or, is she so attached to the child in the pram, she cannot be parted from her? Catherine, another sister and Jeanne's favorite, who is a young schoolteacher and has started to cough up a little blood, wants to know.

Unlikely.

Probably, Jeanne, a simple girl, feels it is her duty.

A Catholic, Jeanne is deeply religious.

But Peru?

Maybe she has simply misunderstood.

Misunderstood the way everyone else at the time has.

The British call it the Phoney War.

The French, *la drôle de guerre.*

For eight months, from September 1939 to May 1940, nothing much happens. Although the European powers have declared war on one another, none of them has yet launched a significant attack. Everyone is waiting —waiting for the German troops to march into Belgium, the Netherlands and Luxembourg. Nonetheless, the Atlantic Ocean is already mined and ships no longer cross it with an assurance of safety—take, for example, HMS *Courageous,* sunk on September 17 with a loss of most of her crew, 518 men. A month later, on October 14, the HMS *Royal Oak* sunk as well, with an even greater loss, of 833 men.

We three cross the Atlantic in July on board the SS *Exeter.* A ten-ton single-funnel cargo liner built by American Export Lines, the ship makes several risky round trips in 1940 and 1941 between Lisbon and New York, transporting thousands of refugees. Like, no doubt, the other refugees, we have left behind most of our belongings—the silver, the china, the paintings, even the elegant pram, which, in any case, I will soon outgrow. (Interesting to note, however, that during the war, the main part of the Silver Cross factory was requisitioned by the Air Ministry and, instead of making prams, it produced over sixteen million parts for Spitfire airplanes.) Photographs taken on the deck of the SS *Exeter* show

my mother, dressed in white shorts, leaning against the
ship's rail; on her head, tilted at a jaunty angle, is the
ship captain's cap. In another, wearing an adult life pre-
server that covers me from head to toe, I sit on the lap
of a young man who, obviously, is not my father. There
are a few snapshots of smiling passengers—unknown
women and children—and finally a photo of the captain
himself. He, too, is smiling, because, perhaps, he has
only just recovered his cap from my mother, and he is
wearing it. There are no photos of Jeanne.

No one knew how long the war would last.

Jeanne cannot have had the faintest idea how long she
will stay in Lima, Peru, a city she has never heard of and
where, during that entire time, those very, very long five
years, she will be completely cut off and receive no letters
nor, for that matter, any news from her family and where,
by the end of the war, she will not have a clue whether any
of them are alive or dead—imagine! A city where it never
rains, a city where it is always hot, exceedingly hot; a
city where there are frequent earthquakes (a particularly
devastating one—8.2 on the Richter scale—which causes
massive damage to the city and nearly destroys the prin-
cipal cathedral in Lima, occurs in 1940, only a few weeks
before she arrives), and where most earthquakes occur in

the middle of the night so that Jeanne has to quickly get
out of bed with just enough time to put on her glasses
but not enough time to get dressed or put on a dressing
gown, and run into my room to wake and get me out
of bed so that, together, we can stand in the doorway
of the room, said to be the safest place in the house; a
city, a country, where she does not speak the language—
Spanish—a city and a country where she knows no one.
Absolutely no one. Not a single other soul. A country
and a city where, during those five years, she will not
learn to speak much Spanish—only a few rudimentary
phrases to get by—and where she will not meet anyone
except for perhaps a few other foreign nannies and the
Spanish servants in the house—the cook, the gardener,
the maid, the part-time chauffeur, all of whom look down
on her, make fun of her. Her timid ways, her pale skin
and thick glasses, her starched and spotless uniform,
all of which they construe as unfriendly and snobbish,
her not joining in with their jokes and complaints in the
kitchen, which, anyway, she has difficulty understanding, her not eating their spicy food, the fried beans, the
tough roasted corn, her keeping herself to herself.

How lonely she is!

To compensate, she looks after me with a concen-
tration and an attention that I still vividly remember and
can almost physically feel, like a presence. She hardly

ever leaves my side—only at night, while I sleep, and on her day off, Wednesday.

We live in the upscale Miraflores district of Lima, in a rented house that has a large garden surrounded by a high stone wall, topped with sharp bits of broken glass. The garden is full of tall red flowers—gladioli. I once lop off all their heads and although, initially, I lie and blame the rabbits, in the end, I confess and get a hard slap in the face from my father, then almost a stranger to me. By then, too, I am five years old and I should know better. The war nearly over, my father has only recently joined us in Lima after spending time first, in a French internment camp for German and Austrian nationals in the Loire Valley, in France, then in North Africa, in the Foreign Legion: this last move not inspired by any spirit of derring-do or romance but rather made out of desperation and to keep from being deported back to Germany—but that is another, very different story. Now, he and my mother argue a great deal. I can hear their angry voices in the bedroom.

No one knew how long the war would last.

True, in the back of the garden, next to the kitchen, there are rabbits. A cage full of them. The rabbits are unusually large and belong to the cook and she raises them to sell and to eat. She feeds them leftover food and dandelion greens. I become fond of one rabbit, a brown one, and name him Pépé. Every day, I take Pépé out of the cage and fondle and pat him. One day, of course, Pépé is gone.

The cook, the maid, the gardener, and the chauffeur always talk about thieves—how, here, in Lima, all the thieves need to do is climb over the garden walls, at night, to rob the houses of the rich. They give examples: only two weeks ago, So-and-so only two houses down, the gardener says, pointing, was robbed. All the jewelry, all the silverware was taken. Another house, one directly in back of ours, the maid joins in, while the people were out—out at a movie, for only a few hours—but when they got home, every piece of furniture, the paintings, the curtains, everything was gone. My mother and her friends talk about how unreliable the servants are and how they are certain the servants are robbing them.

I am more afraid of thieves than I am of earthquakes.

Jeanne! I call out, crying, in the middle of the night if I am having a nightmare and she comes running into my room.

Ma petite chérie is what she calls me as she takes me in her arms and rocks me until I am comforted. It is then, too, in my darkened bedroom, that she talks about her family in Brittany and describes her brothers and sisters to me.

Tell me again about Annick, I beg her.

Annick is the naughty one, Jeanne begins. One day, instead of going to the *boulangerie* to buy bread the way she was told to, Annick . . .

Close your eyes, Jeanne says to me.

And tell me about Daniel, I say. I don't admit to having a crush on Daniel.

Oh, Daniel, Jeanne whispers to me, you should see him. All the girls are in love with Daniel . . .

Jeanne even kisses me, once, twice, on the cheek, before I fall asleep.

But most of the time Jeanne is strict rather than affectionate; she is a disciplinarian. Rarely do I dare disobey her. If I try to play a trick or fool her in a silly way, she is not amused. For instance, I remember how once—and looking back, this event is so out of character, I am tempted to think I have made it up—while walking in the street with her one day, I notice a dog turd lying on the ground, brown, fresh, still steaming and perfectly formed. Look, I tell Jeanne, *une saucisse*, and, leaning down, I stretch out my hand as if I am going to pick it up. Yanking me hard by the arm—so hard, she leaves a red mark—Jeanne says she is going to tell my mother.

Looking back, I think Jeanne is humorless.

But then what does she have to laugh about?

Those Wednesdays?

What is there for a young French nanny who speaks little Spanish to do by herself in Lima on Wednesday?

In the morning, first thing, dressed in a dark skirt, a cotton, long-sleeved blouse, sensible brown shoes, Jeanne leaves the house to go to Mass. She goes to a red stone church called La Ermita, located in the Barranco district of Lima a few miles from Miraflores, which means that she has either to take public transportation, the crowded, dirty bus, or, if the part-time chauffeur is not occupied with driving my mother or, later, my father, beg a ride from him. The church, originally a fisherman's shrine, feels right to her. A miracle occurred there—something to do with fishermen lost at sea in the fog who see a light. The light came from the cross on the church steeple and it guided the fishermen back to the safety of land. On her knees, on the cold stone floor, surrounded by burning candles, faded flowers and the ornately decorated plaster statues of saints, Jeanne, a scarf tied around her head, her eyes closed, prays for the safety of her family back in Brittany. Such a long time since she has seen any of them, she often has a hard time trying to imagine what her brothers and sisters look like. The younger ones, especially, Jacqueline, Didier and Nicolas must have changed and grown a lot since she has last seen them. No longer children, they are teenagers—Jacqueline is sixteen now, and Didier fourteen and—do they do well in school? Are they obedient to their parents? Do they help out at home—milking the cow, feeding the chickens? And what about her father? Is there enough petrol for him to still take out the boat named after her mother—*Marie-Pauline*—to fish? And the others? Has Daniel married Suzanne as he hoped to? Perhaps they have a child already—Jeanne smiles to herself at the thought. Is Catherine still teaching school? She can almost hear how the little village children call out excitedly when they see her—*maîtresse, maîtresse!* And Annick? Has she dyed her hair red the way she always threatens she will? Again, Jeanne smiles. She also thinks about her mother Marie-Pauline, whom she loves very much. All these questions and she prays hard to soon get some answers for them. Getting up from her knees on the floor, she lights a candle for each one of them.

Then does she go to confession?

Mon père, j'ai péché . . .

What sins can Jeanne possibly have to confess?

That she lost her patience with me, when, instead of getting out, I was splashing around in the tub, the water already gone cold, and she spanked my fat little *derrière*?

She pretended not to understand when the cook told her to keep an eye on the water boiling for rice on the stove while she stepped outside to feed the rabbits and the water boiled over?

She let the part-time chauffeur kiss her last Wednesday on the way back from La Ermita but stopped him when he tried to touch her breasts.

Non, non, Hermano, she tells him as she pushes away his hand.

Laughing, Hermano leans past Jeanne and puts his hand against the door handle, thus forcibly, not letting her out of the car.

Un beso, Hermano demands in return for removing his hand and allowing her to open the car door.

Does it happen again the following Wednesday?

No.

It happens again in another way a month later, on a Saturday while my mother is away for a few days visiting Machu Picchu with her North American friends. My father has not yet arrived in Lima and the other servants may or may not be in the house. It is at night and I am in bed and asleep. Jeanne is sitting in the room we call the nursery, which is on the ground floor, off the kitchen; she is knitting a sweater for one of her brothers, for handsome Daniel—but Daniel, unbeknownst to her, has already been dead for quite some time from typhoid fever he contracted in a German prisoner-of-war camp; and not just he, but also her favorite sister, Catherine, who hemorrhaged to death several months ago, and, last year, Jeanne's father, too, died—as she listens to the radio.

The program is in English—it could be the BBC—and Jeanne only understands a few words: a word here like *invasion* or a word there like *bombardment*.

Hola! Hermano, the part-time chauffeur, says to her as he walks into the nursery.

Looking up from her knitting, Jeanne opens her mouth but does not answer him.

Hola, Jeanne! he says again and starts to laugh.

Is he drunk?

She is afraid all of a sudden.

Hermano walks over to where she is sitting listening to the radio and, bending down so that his face is directly level with hers, he makes a loud kissing sound with his lips. Then Hermano shouts something she does not understand.

Not quite true. She understands the word *puta*.

His breath reeks of *pisco*.

Jeanne holds up the knitting needles tight against her chest and, Hermano, as if he could read her mind, grabs them out of her hands and throws the needles, the ball of wool and the half-finished sweater for Daniel across the room. She hears the steel needles hit the wooden floor at the same moment that Hermano, with a backhand blow of his hand, knocks off her glasses and they, too, fall on the floor. And they break.

Poor Jeanne.

* * *

The only school I remember going to in Lima is a small private kindergarten run by an English lady that, after only a few weeks, shuts down because one of the students has contracted scarlet fever. Instead, Jeanne teaches me how to knit, how to sew and embroider. I embroider lots of doilies and half a dozen shoe bags for my mother who, in Lima, has acquired many pairs of high-heel, open-toed sandals that show off her pretty feet. (Later, my mother likes to tell the story of how she was at the movies in Lima one night, and how sitting in the theater she had taken off her shoes when all of a sudden there was an earthquake and everyone got up from their seats and ran out of the theater while she still sat there groping in the dark with her feet trying to find her shoes until the man she was at the movies with shouted at her: "Anna! Come on. Leave your shoes," and she had had to leave off trying to find her shoes and had to run out of the theater in her bare feet. Then, the funny thing, my mother continues, is that when the earthquake was over and she and the man she was with returned to their seats in the theater, the very same seats they had before, she still could not find her shoes. She looked everywhere for them but the shoes were nowhere to be found. The shoes were gone.) All year long in Lima, my mother's legs are tanned and she paints both her finger- and toenails red and wears a matching bright lipstick that leaves a stain on the cigarettes she smokes as she talks on the telephone, making arrangements to meet with her friends—most of them Americans. North Americans who are stationed in Lima. Her best friend is from Miami and the wife of a Panagra pilot. Like my mother, she is tall and blonde. My mother and the wife of the Panagra pilot, I hear people say, could be twin sisters. Gorgeous twin sisters! My mother's real sister is a doctor and during all the time my mother lives in Lima, she, like Jeanne, receives no letter nor any news from her family. Only when the war is over and she returns to France does she learn that her sister is dead.

Nearly every day, my mother plays golf and bridge at the Lima Country Club. On Sunday afternoons, she watches the polo matches there. One Sunday, a few weeks after my fifth birthday and a few weeks before my father is due to arrive in Lima, because Jeanne is not well—all morning, she has been vomiting—and it is both the cook's and maid's day off, and, since the alternative is for my mother to stay home, she takes me to a polo match. I have to behave, she warns, and not wander off but stay next to her at all times. I have to hold her hand, she says. We watch the match standing directly on one

side of the polo field, the side where the wives and friends
of the players stand and where the grooms hold extra
horses and equipment while, at times, no more than a
few feet away, the game is being played. Horses gallop
toward us, charge us, or so it seems, until, at the very
last possible moment, snorting, their hooves clattering,
the riders shouting, the horses stop short, wheel around,
do an intricate quick dance of balance and of changing
leads in midair on their slender bandaged legs, and gallop
off again in another direction as their riders swing their
mallets dangerously close to our heads. It is a hot day, the
sun shines directly overhead, and my mother and I are
wearing hats—she, a large straw hat, and I, an ugly cotton
one. Once or twice, when the horses come galloping over
to us, I am sprayed with flecks of sweat from their necks
and, for some reason, this pleases me and I try to lick the
sweat off my face with my tongue. Looking down, my
mother frowns and says something I do not catch. Then
she takes out a handkerchief from her purse and hands
it to me but, instead of using it, I let the handkerchief
drop to the ground and stand on it so my mother won't
notice. Each time, between games, when the riders ride
over to where we are standing to change their horses, one
of the riders, before dismounting, stops briefly and leans
down to speak to my mother. The rider's arms are dark
and muscular and his teeth are very white.

Sí. Bueno. My mother answers, laughing.

After he dismounts, the rider takes off his helmet and wipes his forehead with a red kerchief, then, taking the bottle his groom hands him, he drinks a swallow from it and spits out another. I watch, shocked—spitting, I know, is forbidden—but I don't say anything to my mother. He is wearing a green shirt and on the back of it is the number 1. Taking the reins of his new, fresh horse, a gray one this time, he mounts it with a single leap—a leap like a cat's—and before he is settled in the saddle or has his feet in the stirrups, the horse is already turning, moving toward the field in anticipation at the same time that the rider waves his mallet at my mother.

This happens three or four times.

When the game is finished, the rider again rides over to my mother but, instead of dismounting, he reins in his horse and, pointing to me with his whip, says, *La niña.*

My mother starts to shake her head but I have already let go of her hand and am reaching up to pat the horse's wet neck. Leaning down, the rider picks me up and, in one effortless motion, sets me down in front of him on the horse's neck. The horse, sensing a foreign presence, shakes his head up and down, and the rider speaks sharply to him at the same time that he gives him a slight flick with his whip as we trot off onto the empty polo field.

Manuel! I hear my mother call out.

Manuel has his arm firmly around my waist as I bounce uncomfortably on the horse's neck, but I don't mind. I laugh.

Also, my cotton hat has come untied and falls to the ground and I am secretly glad that he makes no move to retrieve it.

Manuel! my mother calls out again. Already, she sounds far away.

Soon after, Hermano is arrested for drunken driving and spends a couple of nights in jail and I overhear my mother, on the phone, tell her North American friends that it serves him right because, anyway, she never quite trusted him or his driving and she hopes that this will teach him a lesson. My father arrives in Lima and, to keep busy and out of argument's way, during the last few months of the war, he takes up golf. One day, he manages to hit a hole in one, apparently a cause for celebration, and, in accordance with the customs of the Lima Country Club, he is obliged to buy everyone in the clubhouse a glass of Johnnie Walker scotch whiskey—including one for Manuel, who happens that day to be standing, still wearing his jodhpurs and mud-caked riding boots, at the bar. When, at last, the war is over and it is time for us to go home, Jeanne, who by then is no longer able to properly button up her starched and spotless uniform—instead, she wears a loose, rough cotton housecoat she has purchased at the outdoor market located a few blocks from La Ermita—tearfully tells my mother that instead of going back to Brittany, she will stay on in Pérou, and, thus, as, years earlier, her grandparents had then thought it more than likely, she disappears.

Sure and Gentle Words

In 1911, Professor Solomon died falling out of a speeding train. Was it an accident or a suicide? Or murder? No one has ever been able to determine. Felix—for that was his Christian name, which, as everyone knows, means "happiness" in Latin—was thirty-one years old and taught philology at the University of Bonn. His lectures on comparative linguistics were well attended and his doctoral thesis on the diachronic development in epic fiction had recently been published to much acclaim.

Felix was dark, handsome and had a roving eye. More than once, he was accused by a disapproving colleague of having had a dalliance with a female student—usually, a blonde student. In fact, one such blonde student whose name was Ursula but was known by her friends and classmates as Uli, happened to be on the train from which Felix either jumped, fell or

was pushed. But Uli denied—vehemently shaking her
pretty yellow head—having been aware of Professor
Solomon's presence on the train. *Nein, nein,* she told
the authorities, she did not have the faintest idea and,
of course, had she seen him, she would have right away
greeted him as wasn't he her very own professor at the
university? She, Uli claimed, was on her way to visit
relatives at their country estate and was sitting in her
compartment—several other people were in the compartment with her and they all, no doubt, could vouch
for her presence—and she was absorbed in her book.
Yes, *The Odyssey* in, of course, Greek, for had she not
just said that she was Professor Solomon's pupil?—one
of his star pupils she thought privately to herself with
a certain amount of pride—when, all of sudden, the
train, in the middle of nowhere, a field of some kind
with cows munching contentedly in it, with a terrible
shriek of brakes, came to a stop so abruptly that the
book on her lap fell to the floor.

Felix was married at the time. His wife, Adele, his second cousin once removed, was, like him, an assimilated
Jew. She was a self-reliant, uncomplaining woman, nearsighted and no beauty. She had grown up on a large
family estate in Pomerania and was fond of describing

the details either remembered or invented of her life as a child there: the all-white roses her mother grew in the garden, the mean little pony she was made to ride, a disturbingly gory painting attributed to Delacroix that hung in the somber dining room. Her descriptions also brought to life her sisters: Margaret, the plump, kind one, Friederike, the beautiful, arrogant one, and the spoiled baby, Elizabeth, to say nothing of the much indulged and admired handsome brother, Waldemar, and, finally, plain, rigid Miss Tennyson, the English governess.

Felix and Adele had two children: a boy named Waldemar (named after Adele's brother) and called Walli for short, and a girl, Sonia. Walli was two years old at the time of his father's death and would not remember him; Sonia was older and did. Although he was a loving husband—if, at times, unfaithful—and a kind father—if, at times, distracted—Felix's true passion was epic poetry. Specifically, the poetry of Homer and Hesiod. And, notwithstanding the difficulty of fixing the poets' dates with any certainty—the issue being complicated by the fact that their poems were originally composed orally— Felix was obsessed with their chronology. After studying both the external criteria (comparing the work with historical and archaeological records) and the internal criteria (similar themes, phraseology and unusual diction), he was convinced—despite the more widely held opinion—that Hesiod was the older of the two and—this was a riskier stretch—that the poets were related.

Coincidentally, the passage Uli was reading on the train on that fateful day was the one in which Odysseus angrily responds to Euryalus for ridiculing him on his appearance by arguing that the gods bestow different gifts on different men, but that the eloquent man is especially to be envied and is regarded as a god as he makes his way through the city. Exactly like Professor Solomon, Uli, at the time, could not help but think, recalling how persuasive and articulate his arguments to the class had been as he pointed out the similarity between that passage and the one in *Theogony* where Hesiod speaks of prudent kings who, with their sure and gentle words, are quickly able to end disputes among their people. "Sure and gentle words"—was that not the way she might describe those used by Professor Solomon to seduce her? In spite of herself, Uli had felt herself blushing at the memory of her naked self in bed with the professor, also naked, and, looking up from her book, she glanced around the compartment to see if any of her fellow passengers noticed. Sure enough, the stout woman sitting across from her holding a large, black leather purse tightly to her chest, who until now had appeared to be sleeping, was staring at her intently. Seconds before the train came to its abrupt, shrieking stop, Uli stuck out her tongue at her.

Uli told no one of her affair with Professor Solomon—no one except her miniature white poodle. She whispered her secret into his rank pink ear and the little poodle, as, no doubt, a sign of approval, began feverishly to lick her hand.

Nor, despite the fact that she was engaged soon to be married to the son of a wealthy Prussian officer, did she feel guilty.

And it had begun innocently enough with Professor Solomon sitting behind his desk in his office listening as she spoke about how, in the world of Homer, the most important quality dramatized by his heroes is glory.

Kleos, getting up from his chair and coming to stand next to her, Professor Solomon said.

While Hesiod, Uli continued, describes a world where humans behave according to the laws of gods.

Dikê, Professor Solomon said, putting his hand on Uli's shoulder.

Homer rarely intrudes in the narrative whereas Hesiod inserts himself . . . Uli could feel herself blushing and her voice trailed off.

*   *   *

A few days before the accident occurred on the train, Uli went to be fitted for her wedding dress. Standing on a stool in front of the full-length mirror while the dressmaker was making adjustments to the lace dress—specifically letting out the waist as, inexplicably, Uli had gained weight—Uli fainted. A doctor was summoned and he quickly confirmed what Uli already knew.

At first, she refused to divulge the child's paternity but, in the end, due to her parents' insistent questions and threats she eventually relented on the condition that they not tell the son of the wealthy Prussian officer, to whom she was engaged. Although Uli's father threatened to confront Felix and her mother wept, in the end, her parents decided it was too late to take action. Instead, they would make an excuse about the fragility of her nerves and the restorative qualities of country air and Uli would be banished to the estate of impoverished but discreet relatives where she would deliver the child, immediately give it up, then marry as arranged.

From time to time, Felix suffered from gout. The pain began in his big toe, then spread to the heel of his foot. This attack began in the middle of the night waking him and, unable to bear even the pressure of the linen sheet, Felix kicked off the bedclothes, thus waking up Adele.

Getting out of bed and putting on her robe, Adele went downstairs and prepared a cold water compress that she applied to Felix's foot while he moaned and twisted and turned in the bed. In the morning, she gave Felix apple juice laced with vinegar and several drops of morphine to drink—a home remedy—which he swallowed making a face. As yet, the pain had not abated. His foot hurt like the devil, making Felix nearly senseless.

What day is it today? he managed to ask Adele. Is today the day I have to take the train to Hamburg?

No, today is Wednesday.

Relieved, Felix sank back on to the pillows and shut his eyes. Soon the morphine would take effect but he would have to cancel his class.

He could hardly think straight. He confused his appointment at the bank in Hamburg to discuss how best to invest his dwindling account with what he had assigned—the number of occurrences per thousand lines of enclitics in Hesiod's *Hymns?* or the number of occurrences of proclitics in the *goldmark?*

Not once did he think of Uli.

Earlier, he in fact had begun a letter to her—a letter he was careful to hide from Adele inside the pages of *The Odyssey*—telling Uli that not only did he have to cancel their next meeting as he had to take the train to Hamburg but also explaining in the kindest possible terms that although he would never forget her or forget their time together, their affair must come to an end. Fortunately, Adele never came across the letter but, years later, Sonia, who had begun to study Greek in school and was searching through her father's books for one to read, did. Afraid her mother might find it, Sonia threw the letter into the fireplace and, at the very moment she was lighting a match to it, her brother, Walli, walked into the room. Doubtless thinking this was a secret of Sonia's he might use to tease her, Walli, laughing, snatched up the burning letter. Sonia eventually forgot about the letter except for, from time to time, at odd disjunctive moments much later in her life—driving down an unfamiliar road at night or waiting alone at a train station—she was reminded again of her father's illicit affair and she wondered what had become of Uli. Walli, on the other hand, who had kept the letter and was often accused of having too vivid an imagination, *always* wondered.

On the train on the way to her relatives' country estate, Uli had brought along her little white poodle in a basket that she had placed on the seat beside her. When the train made its unexpected and sudden lurching stop, both the book she was reading and the basket fell to the floor and the poodle ran off. In the confusion that followed—compartment doors were flung open, people ran back and forth in the corridors shouting—the little white poodle disappeared.

Wolfie! Wolfie! Uli repeatedly shouted, becoming more and more agitated. After leaping off the train, it was easy for her to imagine how the poodle was running heedless and crazed and in danger of being trampled by the cows in the field. Determined to rescue him, she pushed open the heavy carriage door and, hiking up her skirt and shutting her eyes, she jumped.

An elderly conductor, who was standing on the ground next to the halted train gently helped Uli back to her feet. Her knees were scraped and she was in tears.

Only then did she notice that farther back down the railroad tracks, next to the embankment, their backs turned to her, a group of men were covering up someone —Uli caught a glimpse of a pair of brown boots—with a dark blanket.

After Uli had delivered the baby—not without certain difficulties resulting from a breech birth—and the baby was properly disposed of, she married the son of the wealthy Prussian officer as planned. Karl was not a bad sort. He was proud of Uli—of her blonde good looks and of her erudition. Often, in the evenings after dinner, he had her read to him in Greek. Although he did not understand a word of what she read, Karl claimed to like the sound of the words and the sound of his wife's voice. Humoring him, Uli obliged, translating the text as she read—frequently adding and embellishing although, mostly, this was not necessary. Not surprisingly, Karl much preferred Homer, whose tales celebrate heroic figures and their military exploits, while he found Hesiod, who sermonized on the need to work hard, dull.

With nothing to fear now that Professor Solomon was dead, Uli nevertheless was curious to know if Karl suspected her of an earlier attachment—her loss of virginity she had attributed to a horseback riding accident. And, at times, too, perversely, she was tempted to confess to Karl—not that he might forgive her but to establish herself in his eyes not merely as a wife and mother of his children, but as someone with a past, someone who had had an adventure. Thus, Uli spoke often and quite freely to Karl how she always looked forward to Wednesday, the day of Professor Solomon's lectures, and how she would not forget them. The two hours he spoke flew by, she told Karl, and were, for her, more like ten minutes, and never once during that time did she glance down at the gold pocket watch hanging from the belt at her waist. Also, she could not write down her notes fast enough—dipping her pen over and over into the inkwell. Afterward, her hand so stiff, she could hardly button up her coat to go home.

Emboldened by her own descriptive powers, Uli went on to tell Karl how trim and handsome Professor Solomon looked in his black frock coat and starched shirt with the high collar as he stood in front of the classroom. On and on—tempting fate or Karl's patience—she continued to describe Felix's thick moustache and his piercing black eyes, as she closed her own blue ones for a moment to allow herself to remember how Felix had looked in bed. Karl, however, did not appear particularly interested in Professor Solomon or in his looks. His remarks to Uli on the subject made it clear that he pictured Felix differently—if he pictured him at all—as a frail, gray-haired old man, which needless to say irritated and further emboldened her.

Before Felix, Uli had never seen a man naked. An only child, she had no brothers or sisters and the reproductions of statues of the Greek and Roman gods she studied at school only whetted her appetite. As for the all-too-secret act of intercourse, that, too, was a mystery that she wanted to solve—her only brush with sex, prior to her affair, was having her little white dog, his penis a glistening pink, try to hump her leg. So that, although she had had little idea what to expect, her eagerness to learn—and who better to teach her than Professor Solomon?—did much to allay her anxiety and shock when Felix took off the black frock coat and the starched shirt with the high collar and stood naked in front of her. Nor was she shocked by the thick black hair that covered his back, his arms and legs, his chest and stomach and, more thickly, his groin. In fact, later, Karl naked would shock her more. He was blond, hairless and not circumcised. Until her own son was born, this latter anomaly had puzzled her but she had not dared to question Karl on this delicate subject.

When the war broke out, Karl immediately joined the Eighth Army commanded by General Maximilian von Prittwitz and was sent to the Prussian front to fight the Russians. Less than three weeks later he was dead. Killed on either August 19 or early on the morning of August 20, 1914, at Gumbinnen, the first major German offensive, Karl would not live to see what would turn out to be a famous and defining victory for the Germans, the Battle of Tannenberg. Nor would he live to learn about the 170,000 Russian casualties or hear how the Russian general Alexander Samsonov shot himself in the head after his defeat so as not to face Tsar Nicholas II.

Uli received a single letter from the field. The letter was postmarked Allenstein, East Prussia, and it arrived several days after Karl died.

August 17, 1914. Königsberg

Dearest Uli,

A victory today! We beat back the Russians at Stallupönen! As yet, I myself have not seen any action and we have, for the time being, been ordered to withdraw. I am writing you as I sit underneath a large oak tree in the Zulkiner Forest. It is a clear night and I can see a few stars shining above the canopy of leaves. Except for the sound of occasional stamping and snorting from the horses who are tethered nearby, it is very quiet and, for the moment, peaceful so that I find it difficult to imagine battle—the noise of cannons, artillery, gunfire. Instead, I am thinking of you, my darling wife, and I like to imagine I can hear your sweet voice as you read to me in the evening. I also cannot help but be reminded of Odysseus and of his military exploits and glory.

The letter continues by reminding Uli of some household duties, such as the hiring of a new servant, the payment of certain bills, and, finally, urging her to escape the summer heat of the city and visit his family in the country and not to forget to give them his best regards. The letter ends with Karl sending fond kisses to

their twin infants, Jasper and Charlotte, and his bound-
less and eternal love to Uli.

Soon after the war, Adele left Bonn and went to live in
Koblenz with Walli and Sonia as she was able to find
work in a publishing house that had begun again to
print medical texts. She found two furnished rooms on
the second floor of a widow's house—she shared the
kitchen with her and had to go outside to use the toilet.
The woman's husband had died as had her son, at Ypres,
and life had become hard for her. Hard for Adele as well.
A professor's pension was not enough to live on and, by
then, the mark had begun its terrible plunge and soon
was worth almost nothing.

The American occupying forces—part of the Second Infantry Division that had fought under Major General Lejeune in the Argonne Forest, marking the end of
the war—were stationed in Koblenz; their barracks were
located on the banks of the Rhine. The insignia stitched
on the soldiers' uniform sleeves—an Indian wearing a
feather headdress inside a five-pointed star—was quite
unusual and Walli, who was eleven at the time and had a
tendency to embellish and dramatize, persuaded himself
and his schoolmates that the soldiers of the Second Infantry Division fought with tomahawks. Adele felt sorry

for the poor soldiers. There was nothing for them to do in Koblenz; they were bored and they wanted to go home. The townspeople resented them of course.

In the mornings, Adele walked to work. The publishing house was located on the banks of the Rhine and every morning an American soldier on a spirited sorrel mare would ride past her. Adele got accustomed to seeing the soldier, sitting straight and tall on his mare, and soon he, too, began to politely touch his cap and say good morning to her. One day, as he was riding by, Adele's straw hat, in a sudden gust of wind, blew off her head and blew directly in front of the mare's head, causing the mare to shy violently and causing the soldier, who had one hand raised up in the air ready to touch his cap, to be thrown. While the soldier was slowly getting to his feet—he had hurt his ankle—Adele walked the few yards to where the mare was standing by the side of the road, placidly eating grass, and took hold of the reins and adjusted the saddle that had slipped down—had she not learned how thanks to the mean little pony she had been obliged to ride as a child?—and led the mare back to the soldier. Resting his hand heavily on Adele's shoulder for balance and grimacing with pain, the soldier managed to get back in the saddle.

The soldier's name was John Murray, but he was known as Jack. As soon as he was sufficiently recovered from his sprained ankle, Jack, although engaged to be married to his high school sweetheart back home in Virginia, began an affair with Adele. He was not in love with Adele, but he was lonely and grateful. Adele, on the other hand, did fall in love with Jack. Jack was blond and handsome and she liked his courteous ways and liked the unfamiliar, southern inflection to his voice when he spoke—so different from the English she had learned from Miss Tennyson. Also, Adele had not had sex since Felix had died. The affair was brief and the sex—where they could have it—proved the main difficulty. On account of the children, Sonia and Walli, as well as her widowed landlady, Adele could not take Jack up to her rented rooms, nor could she go with him to the army barracks. Luckily, it was springtime and the weather was warm and Adele and Jack made love outdoors—in the woods, on a secluded part of the river bank, in a deserted field. Adele hardly seemed to mind the discomfort of lying on her back in damp grass or on an uncomfortable tree root or the other difficulties posed by their clandestine meetings. Once they disturbed a hornets' nest and had to get up and run not to be stung; another time they nearly got caught by a boy riding by on his bicycle; and still another, and this was the last time, a little white dog appeared, seemingly out of nowhere and with no visible owner and, circling the prone couple, barked furiously at them the entire time Jack and Adele were making love. And, every time, too, Adele could not help but briefly wonder to herself what Felix would have thought if he could see his staid, practical wife with her breasts bare, her skirt hiked up to her chin, her glasses askew on her nose, taking such pleasure.

Uli married again, and, with her second husband, went to live in America. She had several more children, and although a good mother and wife, she nevertheless always thought of Felix as the love of her life. Her defining love. The man against whom she measured all other men—notably, her two husbands. Felix had, at once, been patient, assured and adoring. He had been careful to make sex for Uli comfortable and pleasurable. In turn, a willing pupil, she had let him instruct her. She trusted him and learned to feel at ease with herself and with nakedness. And although their affair lasted only a few months and Uli was very young, she often wondered how she had lived for so long in ignorance and without desire.

Sonia, Adele's daughter, married a professor of physics; with her husband, she moved to England. Fortunately,

Adele also was able to go to England before the start of
the Second World War (Friederike, Elizabeth and Waldemar stayed in Germany and were not so fortunate; Miss
Tennyson, the governess, had, of course, left years ago).
Adele went to live with Margaret, the kind plump sister.
Margaret was married to an Englishman and lived on a
farm in Essex. In either 1938 or 1939—Adele could no
longer remember which year—she suffered a detached
retina and was forced to stay in bed, lying immobile on
her back, for several months. In addition, sand bags
were placed around her head to keep her from moving
it. The only thing she remembered clearly of that time—
besides listening to the increasingly distressing news
on the BBC—was Margaret reading out loud to her in
the afternoons. No intellectual, Margaret was nevertheless an avid reader of novels and, of all the novels that
Margaret read to her, Adele's favorite was *Jane Eyre*. The
passage she liked best was the one where Jane first meets
Mr. Rochester on the road to Thornfield Hall and where
Mr. Rochester's horse slips and falls on the ice. Margaret
had to reread this passage twice to Adele.

Walli chose to take quite a different path from that of
his academic father. In 1933, he went to live in Paris,
where he fell in love and where he began to make films.

One of his films begins with a man walking unsteadily in between the cars of a speeding train. The credits are rolling on the screen, which makes it difficult to tell whether the man is in physical pain or so preoccupied with his thoughts—thoughts that may have to do with how similar passages in Homer and Hesiod suggest a relationship—when a young woman with indistinct features but with very blonde hair, her arms outstretched as if to embrace him, comes toward him and so startles him that he loses his footing on the uneven metal couplings that join the two cars and, stumbling against the side door, which is not shut properly, he falls out of the speeding train.